Claudia and the
Phantom Phone Calls

THE BABY-SITTERS CLUB

Claudia and the Phantom Phone Calls

Ann M. Martin

GREY CASTLE PRESS

Library edition:
GARETH STEVENS PUBLISHING

First Grey Castle Edition, Lakeville, Connecticut, September, 1988

Published in large print by arrangement with Scholastic, Inc., New York.

Printed in the U.S.A.

The Library of Congress Cataloging in Publication Data Available.

ISBN 0-0942545-63-X   (lg. print)
ISBN 0-0942545-73-7   (lib. bdg.: lg. print)

This book is for
Brenda Bowen
and
Jean Feiwel
with gratitude

CHAPTER 1

The evening was gloomy and windy, with rain streaming down from heavy clouds that blocked the moon. I thought it was the perfect night to a) curl up with *The Phantom of Pine Hill* — a really spooky Nancy Drew mystery — and the licorice whips I'd hidden in my desk, or b) work on the still life I'd started and daydream about Trevor Sandbourne. But "No," my dad said, "homework first, Claudia," and there's no arguing with Dad. Besides, we have an agreement, my parents and I. The agreement is that if I get all my homework done every night (with someone in my family supervising me), I can continue to take my art classes. More important, I can stay in the Baby-sitters Club.

The Baby-sitters Club is something my friend Kristy Thomas thought up a little while ago at the beginning of seventh grade. Kristy, who lives across the street from me, does a lot of baby-sitting. So do I, Claudia Kishi, and so does Kristy's best friend, Mary Anne Spier, who lives next door to Kristy. So Kristy had this idea that the three of us should get together to form a group of baby-sitters, advertise ourselves, and have a little business, which is just what we did. Plus, we asked a new friend of mine, Stacey McGill, to join, which *she* did. The Baby-sitters Club is working really well. People know about us and call us all the time, and each of us has more jobs now than before the Baby-sitters Club, so it was important that I be allowed to stay in it. But I almost blew it when the school sent a letter home to my parents saying that I wasn't working up to potential and stuff like that. My parents are used to those letters — they get them about twice a year — but what they hadn't expected to find out was that I had done almost none of my homework since school started. That was when Mom and Dad laid down the law.

The thing about homework is that it is just so boring I can barely concentrate on it. And it's useless. Who cares whether $>$ means greater than or less than, or what $\times$ equals? (Besides, why bother finding out, since $\times$ equals something different every time?) The only school thing I like to do is read, and the teachers even take the fun out of that. They don't care that

I can almost always solve a mystery before the detective in the story can. They just care that I don't know what an adverb is.

None of this would be so bad if it weren't for Janine. Janine is my sister. She's fifteen and a real-and-true genius. Her I.Q. is 196, which is above average (100), and above above-average (120), and even above the cutoff point for geniusness, which is 150. Actually, I'll tell you a secret. My I.Q. is also above average. Everyone is amazed, since I can barely spell, but that's why my parents and teachers come down so hard on me. I'm smart, but I'm not a good student. They say if I'd just *Pay Attention* and *Concentrate*, I could do fine in school. But who cares? I'd never live up to Janine.

You have no idea what it's like to have a genius for an older sister (unless, of course, you have one yourself). You can't even say the simplest thing to her. Yesterday morning all I did was go, "Janine, it's cold out. Mom wants you to close your window before you leave for school," and you know what she said? She said, "I find it fascinating that in our society we attempt to regulate the temperature of our environment rather than our bodies. It's so much more difficult and it's highly inefficient. Primitive peoples and peoples in various other societies existing today tend toward the mere addition or removal of clothing, while we invite the use of heating units and air conditioners."

I didn't even know there was such a word as *peoples*.

Anyway, to get back to that gloomy evening, Dad said I had to do my homework, and he said it was Mimi's turn to help me. I'm supposed to try to do the work on my own, but one of them sits next to me to keep me from daydreaming, to make sure I do each assignment completely, to see that I follow directions and stuff, and to answer questions if I have them. They're not supposed to do the homework *for* me, but sometimes I can get Janine to give me answers. This is because my dumb homework is *so boring* for her, as she tells me at least twice every time she has to help me, that she'll do anything to speed it along. Well, I'm sorry. I'm sorry I'm not up to trigonomulus, or whatever it is she does. We can't all be scholars.

Mimi, my grandmother, is the best person to help me. She's quiet and softspoken and endlessly patient. My family is Japanese, and Mimi and my grandfather (who died long before I was born) brought my mother to the United States when Mom was just a little girl. Mom has no accent whatsoever (neither does my father, who also came to the United States

4

as a small child), but Mimi has this pleasant, rolling accent that reminds me of a ship at sea. And she is polite, polite, polite, never speaking a harsh word.

I got out my social studies text.

"What do we have between the covers of this book?" asked Mimi, who thinks books are eyes into the hearts and lives of other people (peoples?). She told me so once.

"Social studies," I replied. "We read chapter three in class today. Now we have to answer the discussion questions at the end of the chapter. . . . Mimi, if they're discussion questions, why aren't we discussing them? How come Mr. Miller is making us write them down?"

"I do not know, my Claudia, but if that is the assignment, then you must complete it as your teacher wishes."

"I know." Boy, did I know. A few weeks ago, I would have written down one-word answers or skipped the assignment altogether. Now there was no way out.

I began to write. Mimi looked on, every now and then pointing out a misspelled word or suggesting that I check my punctuation. After social studies came math and then English, and at last I was done. I breathed a sigh that was relief mixed with boredom.

"And what are you going to do now, my Claudia?" asked Mimi.

"Get back to *The Phantom of Pine Hill*," I replied, slapping my English text closed. Mimi knows about my Nancy Drew books, but no one else in the family does. Mom and Dad would tell me to read something more grown-up, and Janine would tell me to read something more worthwhile. (*Her* idea of a really good book, something to curl up with in front of a fire, is *Sources of American Social Tradition*, which at this very moment she's devouring as if she were never going to read again.)

"And what is happening in *The Phantom of Pine Hill*?" asked Mimi.

"Ooh, it's really spooky," I began.

"You like to be scared, my Claudia?"

"Well, yes, I guess so. I mean, when it's just a book, it's fun. Look outside, Mimi. Look at the wind blowing the trees, and the lightning flashing. It's the perfect night to read a mystery."

Mimi smiled. "Spooky. . . . It is almost Halloween," she remarked. "Just a few more weeks."

I nodded. "But I think I'm too old to go trick-or-treating."

"Well, then, you can dress up and help us hand out the candy. I'm sure that is almost as much fun as tricks-and-treats."

Mimi knows how much I like to dress up. It's very important to me. I think clothes make a statement about the person inside them. Also, since you have to get dressed every day, why not at least make it fun? Traditional clothes look boring and are boring to put on. So I never wear them. I like bright colors and big patterns and funny touches, such as earrings made from feathers. Maybe this is because I'm an artist. I don't know. Today, for instance, I'm wearing purple pants that stop just below my knees and are held up with suspenders, white tights with clocks on them, a purple-plaid shirt with a matching hat, my high-top sneakers, and lobster earrings. Clothes like these are my trademark.

I like costumes, too, and I'll really miss being able to show one off this year. But, as Mimi said, I could make one just to wear when I pass out goodies. Maybe I'll dress up as a Smurf. Blue makeup would be fun.

I stood up. "Thanks for helping me, Mimi. I wish you could help me every night."

"I know, my Claudia, but I think it is better to take turns. Some evenings I am busy, and your mother and father like to see your work, too."

"Right." So why does Janine have to help

me? It's because my homework is so boring, no one can stand it for more than one night in a row — even Mimi — and the less often they have to help me, the better (for them).

I was halfway upstairs when I remembered something. I turned around and ran back down to the first floor. "Mimi?" I called.

"Yes, my Claudia?" She was settling down in the den with a fat book.

"I just thought of something. Let's work on your portrait." In my art class, we'd been assigned two projects that semester: One was the still life, and one was a portrait. Both were to be done in oils. Mimi was the subject of my portrait. "Would you mind?" I asked. "We'll just work for half an hour or so."

"That would be fine." Mimi carefully placed a marker in her book. She followed me to my room.

I know artists are supposed to paint in daylight, but between school and baby-sitting, I didn't have many daylight hours left over. I had to settle for painting in my room with every light blazing.

I posed Mimi in the easy chair, adjusted my easel, and got to work. It was the third time Mimi had sat for me, and the painting was really coming along.

"Mimi?" I said after a few minutes. "Tell me

about when you were a little girl in Japan."

Mimi smiled and began the story I'd heard so many times before. She was good at talking without moving around. "We were a family very much like this one," she said. "I lived with my parents, my older sister, and my grandfather — my father's father."

"Mimi," I suddenly interrupted. "did you and your sister get along?"

"Oh, yes," replied Mimi. "My sister was my friend, my dear friend. We studied together and played together. I followed her everywhere and tried to do all the things she did. She was very patient with me."

"Why aren't Janine and I friends?" I asked, frowning at the portrait.

"Being friends takes work," replied Mimi quietly. "To be a good friend you must spend time with someone. You must talk to her and try to understand her. That is how you became friends with Kristy and Mary Anne and Stacey."

"But Janine is impossible to talk to," I protested. "And she never has time for me. Well, hardly ever. She helps me with my homework, but that doesn't count."

"And what about you? Do you have time for your sister?"

"Not very often."

"Someday you will be friends," said Mimi.

I went back to her portrait, and she continued her story. Later, when she had left my room, I got the licorice whips out of my desk and the Nancy Drew book out from under my mattress, where it was hidden, along with a bag of root beer barrels.

I was up to chapter fourteen in *The Phantom*, and it really was pretty exciting. Even so, as I chewed away on the licorice, my thoughts began to wander, and they wandered right to Trevor Sandbourne.

I lowered the book.

Trevor Sandbourne is the most gorgeous boy in the entire seventh grade at Stoneybrook Middle School. And he happens to have the most romantic name in the whole world. Trevor has jet black hair and dark, brooding eyes and freckles on his nose. He walks through the halls looking serious and deep in thought, and he writes poetry for *The Literary Voice*, our school's creative journal. I never dreamed I would fall in love with a poet. The only problem is that Trevor and I don't have any classes together, so we don't know each other at all. He probably doesn't even know I'm alive.

R-r-r-r-ing! The sound of the phone made me jump. I reached for the receiver, wondering if there was just the teensiest chance that Trevor was on the other end.

"Hello?"

"Hi, Claud. It's me."

"Hi, Stacey."

"What are you doing?"

"Thinking about Trevor Sandbourne. What are you doing?"

"Thinking about Sam Thomas." (Sam Thomas is one of Kristy's older brothers, and Stacey has an Immense Crush on him. Personally, I think he's too old for her. He's a freshman in high school.)

I sighed.

Stacey sighed.

"Any Baby-sitters Club calls?" she asked after a moment.

"Nope."

"Really?"

"Really." The headquarters for the club is my bedroom. This is because I'm the only one of the four of us with a phone in my room. Not only that, I have a private number. The Baby-sitters Club meets three times a week in my room and if people call during a meeting, they can reach all four of us at once, so they're bound to get a sitter immediately. As Kristy says, "That's the beauty of the club." Of course, people can call us individually at our homes during other times, plus a number of club calls come in on my line when we're not meeting. When that happens, I'm supposed to take down all the information about the job, like when it is, how many kids there will be, and how late the parents will be out — stuff like that. Then I'm supposed to offer the job to all the club members before calling the client back with a sitter. I'll admit that a few times I've forgotten to do this and have taken the job myself on the spot. But I didn't think it was very nice of Stacey to imply that I was job-hogging.

Stacey sighed again.

"Is anything wrong?" I asked her.

"I just wish I knew more people, that's all."

"You will, Stace. Look, you haven't even been here two months yet. It takes time to make friends." Stacey and her parents had moved to Stoneybrook, Connecticut from New York City in August.

"I guess," she said.

"Maybe you and I could get together with Kristy and Mary Anne on Saturday. I mean, to do something besides have a club meeting. Are you free Saturday?"

"I'm always free," said Stacey.

"Oh, come on, you are not. You get lots of

baby-sitting jobs, and you get to go back to New York with your parents all the time."

"That's not the same as having friends."

"So — let's do something Saturday, okay? I'll call Kristy and Mary Anne."

"All right."

"See you tomorrow, Stace."

" 'Bye."

" 'Bye."

We hung up and I stared out the window at the rain. It wouldn't be easy finding something Mary Anne's strict father would allow her to do, or something Stacey's strict diet would allow *her* to do, but I was determined that we would get together. I'd talk to Kristy and Mary Anne in school the next day.

I went back to *The Phantom of Pine Hill*.

CHAPTER 2

Stacey, Kristy, Mary Anne, and I did get together on Saturday, but we couldn't think of a thing for the four of us to do together. Many Anne wasn't allowed to ride her bike to the mall. Stacey couldn't eat s'mores or ice cream or anything fun. (She has diabetes and has to control very carefully the amount of sugar she takes in each day.) And there was only one movie playing in town and Kristy and I had already seen it.

Se we sat around in Kristy's front yard. We were sprawled all over the place, except for Stacey who was sitting up primly with her legs tucked under her. She wanted to look nice in case Sam should come along or poke his head out the door or something. Mary Anne had the latest edition of *The Stoneybrook News* spread open in front of her, but she wasn't reading it. We were very, *very* bored.

"We could go up in the attic and look through

that trunk of antique toys that Mom got from Grandma's," Kristy suggested.

Stacey and I rolled our eyes. Even though Kristy and Mary Anne are in seventh grade, just like Stacey and I are, they can be very childish. They're not interested in boys or clothes yet, and sometimes they do the weirdest things. Mary Anne still dresses up her stuffed animals. And they even *look* younger than we do. Kristy has long brown hair which she doesn't do much with yet, and big brown eyes which will look great with makeup in a couple of years. She's small for her age. She looks more like a ten-year-old. Mary Anne also has brown eyes and brown hair. Her father makes her wear her hair in braids. I wonder how long that will go on. And both of them wear kind of little-girl clothes — kilts and plain blouses and stuff like that.

Stacey, on the other hand, dresses pretty much the way I do. She's tall and slender and her mother lets her get her blonde hair permed. She looks older than twelve.

"We could try that new cookie pl— " Mary Anne began, than glanced at Stacey and stopped, remembering the diet problem.

"We could rent a movie for your VCR," I said to Stacey.

"Yeah!" said Kristy.

"Yeah!" said Mary Anne.

"The VCR's broken," said Stace.

"Oh."

I picked up a bright yellow maple leaf and twirled the stem between my thumb and forefinger. "I'll tell you guys a secret," I said. "Well, Stacey knows about this, but no one else does."

"How come you already told Stacey?" asked Kristy accusingly.

"I just did, that's all. Okay?"

I saw Kristy and Mary Anne glance at each other and knew what they were thinking — that Stacey and I left them out of things. Well, maybe we did sometimes.

"Do you want to know the secret or not?"

"Yes," said Kristy grudgingly.

"Okay. Well, here it is . . . " I said slowly, trying to drag out the suspense. "I'm in love!"

"Ohh!" said Mary Anne softly.

"You *are?*" cried Kristy at the same time.

"Who with?" asked Mary Anne.

I sighed deeply. "Trevor Sandbourne." I closed my eyes and leaned against the maple tree.

"Trevor Sandbourne?" repeated Kristy.

Mary Anne squinted at me through her reading glasses and pushed one braid behind her shoulder. "Who's he?"

"Only the most gorgeous boy in school."

"I don't think I've heard of him. Is he in our grade?"

"Yup. He's a poet," I said. I tried to describe him.

"Oh!" exclaimed Kristy, right in the middle of my description. "I know who you mean. He's really quiet. He's in my math class. He sits in the row behind me — right next to Alan Gray."

"Oh, you poor thing," I said. "Alan Gray. Ick."

"Yeah," added Mary Anne, sounding pretty disgusted. I mean, pretty disgusted for Mary Anne, which for most people isn't very disgusted at all. See, Mary Anne lives alone with her father who is really, really strict and overprotective. Because of him, Mary Anne is shy and "held-in," if you know what I mean. Mr. Spier thinks that because Mary Anne's mother is dead, he has to go overboard with this careful upbringing, making Mary Anne super-polite and kind of old-fashioned.

"Who's Alan Gray?" asked Stacey, reminding us that she was a newcomer to Stoneybrook.

"Alan Gray," said Kristy witheringly, "is the most disgusting boy in this whole solar system. He's been awful since kindergarten. Probably since birth. And I can tell you it's no picnic having Alan sit right in back of me. Yesterday he told Mr. Peters that I was late for class because I had to go to the doctor for a flea bath."

"That's *awful!*" exclaimed Stacey.

"I know. He really hates me. He doesn't bother anyone else half as much as he bothers me."

"Well, you *are* the only girl who ever fought him back, you know," I pointed out.

"Yeah," said Kristy with a grin.

A slow smile spread across Mary Anne's face as she remembered what we were talking about. Even Mary Anne had thought it was funny.

"*What?*" demanded Stacey, looking frustrated.

"Fifth grade," I began. "That year Kristy, Mary Anne, Alan, and I were all in the same class. Kristy really got Alan. He'd been tormenting us — all the girls, really — for the entire year, and by June we had had it. So one day, Kristy comes to school and all morning she brags about this fantastic lunch her mother has packed: a chocolate cupcake, Fritos, fruit salad, a ham and cheese sandwich, two Hershey's Kisses — really great stuff. Kristy says it's a reward for something or other. And she says the lunch is so great she's got to protect it by keeping it in her desk instead of in the coat room. So, of course, Alan steals the bag out of her desk during the morning. Then at noontime in the cafeteria, he makes this big production out of opening it. He's sitting at the boys' table and they're all crowded around, and us girls are looking on from the next table. Alan is the center of attention, which is just what he wants."

"And just what I wanted," added Kristy.

"Right. So Alan carefully takes all the packages and containers out of the bag and spreads them in front of him. Then he begins to open them. In one he finds dead spiders, in another he finds a mud pie."

"David Michael had made it for me," said Kristy. (David Michael is Kristy's little brother. He was four then.)

"She'd even wrapped up a sandwich with fake flies stuck on it."

Stacey began to giggle.

"It was great," said Mary Anne. "Everyone was laughing. And Kristy had packed a real lunch for herself which she'd kept in the coat room. All afternoon, the kids kept telling her how terrific her trick had been."

"The only bad thing," said Kristy, "is that ever since, Alan has thought he has to bother me constantly in order to keep up his reputation. He's like the plague."

"Thank goodness Trevor isn't like that," I said.

"If he was, you wouldn't have fallen in love with him," Stacey pointed out. She brushed her curly blonde hair out of her eyes.

"That's true. Poets are sensitive and thoughtful."

We fell silent.

Mary Anne flipped idly through *The Stoneybrook News*. "Taylor's is going to have a sale," she announced.

"Mmm." (I had closed my eyes and was trying to conjure up a picture of Trevor in my mind.)

"There was a fire at the mall this week."

"Mmm."

"Everyone's supposed to get flu shots by November."

"Mmm."

"Aughhh!"

Kristy, Stacey, and I jerked to attention.

"What is it? What is it?" I cried.

Mary Anne had turned pale.

With one shaking hand, she pointed at the paper. With the other hand, she held the paper away from her, as if it might bite.

"Is something on the paper?" I shrieked. I

20

jumped away. I absolutely *hate* spiders.

"No, *in* the paper," Mary Anne managed to say.

Kristy grabbed it from her and she and Stacey kneeled on the ground and leaned over the pages Mary Anne had it opened to.

" '*Angry Pig Goes Hog Wild*'?" asked Kristy, reading one of the larger headlines.

"No!" cried Mary Anne.

" '*Depressed Trucker Drives Self Crazy*'?" asked Stacey.

"No!"

"What *is* it, Mary Anne? Just tell us," I shouted. "You're driving *us* crazy."

Mary Anne had calmed down a little. She took the paper back and read: " '*Phantom Caller on Rampage in Mercer.*' " She cleared her throat and glanced at us. Then she began to read again. " 'The thief, whom police have nick-named the Phantom Caller, struck again in Mercer on Tuesday night. Following the pattern of his previous burglaries, he began making phone calls, this time to the home of Thornton and Sophia Granville of 236 Witmer Court, shortly after four P.M. He never spoke, simply hanging up the phone when someone answered. The Granvilles left their home at seven-thirty to attend a meeting of the school board. When they returned at ten-fifteen, they found all of Mrs. Granville's jewelry missing. Nothing else had been taken, despite the fact that a considerable amount of silver, as well as Thornton Granville's famous and very valuable coin collection, were in the house.

" 'This is the sixth home the Phantom Caller has robbed in the past two weeks, and the second home in Mercer. The first four robberies occurred in New Hope.' " Mary Anne stopped reading.

"So what is so scary about that?" asked Stacey. "You should hear what goes on in New York City every day."

"But don't you see?" asked Mary Anne. "He's getting closer and closer to Stoneybrook — to *us*. First New Hope, then Mercer. Stoneybrook is the nearest town to Mercer."

"Well, it's still twenty miles away," I said. "Does he always steal jewelry?"

"Yes," replied Mary Anne. "Just jewelry. It says in the next paragraph that he really knows what he's looking for. Now here's the scary part: He makes those phone calls to find out whether anyone's home. But *some*times if the people don't go out he robs them anyway, and they don't know it until they realize the jewelry's missing. He's *in* the house while they are. He's never hurt anyone, but what do you think he'd do if he met someone face-to-face

22

in the middle of a burglary? Now think about *this*," she went on. "We don't know what kind of jewelry the people we baby-sit for have."

"Oh," said Stacey, "no one around here is as rich as those Granvilles sound."

"But maybe it doesn't matter," said Kristy. "And what if the Phantom Caller were watching the house or something and saw the parents go out. He might go ahead and rob it if he thought just a baby-sitter and a couple of little kids were there."

"I still don't know," said Stacey. "I think you guys are worrying about nothing."

Suddenly I clapped my hand to my mouth. "Oh, my gosh!" I cried.

"What?" the others shouted.

"When I baby-sat for the Marshalls on Wednesday, the phone rang twice and each time I answered it, the caller hung up without saying a word!"

"Oh, no!"

"You're kidding!"

"I think," said Kristy seriously, "that we should hold an emergency meeting of the Baby-sitters Club — *right now*."

CHAPTER 3

The members of the Baby-sitters Club gathered numbly in my bedroom.

"This is *terr*ible," moaned Kristy. "How can we baby-sit under these conditions?"

Nobody said a word. To ease the tension, I took a gigantic chocolate bar out of my notebook, carefully peeled back the wrapper, and offered pieces to Kristy and Mary Anne. I didn't even bother to feel bad that Stacey couldn't eat any. The three of us chewed in silence.

"Look," said Stacey after a while, "I think we're worrying about nothing. The Phantom Caller hasn't even robbed anybody in Stoneybrook, so he's still at least twenty miles away." She turned to Mary Anne. "What makes you so sure he'll come here next? Maybe he'll decide that with the police on his tail he should just clear out and go rob people in Oklahoma."

"That's true," said Mary Anne slowly.

"And in the second place, if anyone we sit for *does* have some fantastic piece of jewelry and the Phantom Caller has heard about it, don't you think *we'd* have heard about it, too? I mean, it wouldn't be any secret then."

"That's true, too," I said, "but . . . well, what if we just happened to be baby-sitting somewhere and a burglar just happened to try to break in? Not the Phantom Caller necessarily, but any burglar? It could happen, you know, and we should be prepared."

"You're right," said Kristy. "Good baby-sitters should be prepared for anything."

"Maybe," said Stacey, "we should arrange a code we could give each other over the phone that would be a signal for the other person to call the police. Let's say I'm baby-sitting for Jamie Newton, and I hear a burglar. Okay. I want to call the police, but I don't want the burglar to *hear* me calling the police, right?"

"Right," said the rest of us.

"So what I do is call Claudia, for example, and I say, 'Hi, it's Stacey. *Have you found my red ribbon?*' and that's a signal that I'm in trouble and need Claudia to call the police."

"Hey, that's a neat idea!" said Kristy.

"Yeah!" agreed Mary Anne. "But how would Claudia know where you are? How would she know where to send the police?"

"That's right. That's a good question, Stace,"
I said, "because what if the burglar were
listening in on an extension? I couldn't just say,
'Okay, I'll call the police. Where are you?' That
wouldn't do you any good at all."

"Aughh! Listening in on an extension! That
is *so* creepy!" screamed Kristy.

"But it could happen," I said. "It happened
in that thriller, *The Night of the Weird.* You
know, the one where they find the baby-
sitter — "

"Stop! Stop! Stop! Don't say any more. I
don't want to know!" cried Kristy.

"All right, but the point is," I said, "that we
should all know where each one of us is sitting
and when."

"Well," said Mary Anne, "there's the record
book."

The record book is where we keep track of
our baby-sitting appointments as well as all
other important club information. Kristy makes
us keep a club notebook, too. Each time we
complete a job, we're supposed to write up
what happened. Then the other club members
will know about any problems with kids or
their families or homes, and know what to
expect the next time they sit for the client.

I should mention here that each of us holds
an office in the Baby-sitters Club. Mary Anne

"What about them?" I countered.

"I think that if we're baby-sitting and anything strange happens — a silent phone call, a funny noise outside, *any*thing — we should rig up some kind of burglar alarm so that at least we'd know if someone tried to break into the house."

For a moment nobody spoke. At last Mary Anne said, "You mean like stacking tin cans in front of a door so that if the door opened, the cans would crash down and alert you?"

"Exactly!" cried Kristy. "That's a good idea." She tore a piece of paper out of my social studies notebook and wrote:

1. *Stack cans in front of door or window (inside).*

"But," she added, "make sure you don't put the stuff where the kids you're sitting for could fall over it. And make sure you put it away before the parents come home."

"Right," we agreed.

"Okay. Other ideas? Claudia?" asked Kristy. She was beginning to sound like some of my teachers.

"No," I said crossly, feeling embarrassed. Then I added, "Do you have any?" realizing Kristy had been doing a lot of talking and is secretary, which is why she was thinking of the record book. Kristy is president, since the club was her idea. I'm vice-president, since the headquarters is my bedroom and I have a private phone. And Stacey is treasurer, since she likes numbers.

"What about the record book?" asked Stacey.

"It's got all the information in it — our appointments, the money we've earned, everything. I could bring it to school every day so we could check the calendar. And during our regular Friday afternoon meetings we coul check it for the weekend. That way each of would be sure to know what the others doing — where they're going to be baby ting."

"That's a good suggestion," said k "except that, as president, I'll take re bility for the book during school. If a happens to it, it'll be my fault."

"You don't have to do that," I s could take turns."

"No, it's easier if the same per has it. I don't mind. So I move t bring it to school everyday."

"I second the motion," said looking relieved.

"Good," said Kristy. "Now glar alarms?"

writing and not much thinking.

There was an awkward silence. Then, "How about a Smell Alert?" said Kristy with a giggle.

Mary Anne and Stacey laughed, but I thought Kristy was sounding pretty childish again.

"What," I demanded, "is a Smell Alert, if I may ask?"

Kristy couldn't stop giggling. "You put something really gross, like garbage, outside the house, where the burglar is bound to step in it. Then when he breaks in, you smell him before you even hear him. A Smell Alert!"

I had no intention of laughing. All I said was, "You know, a burglar *could* be a woman. It doesn't have to be a man."

"Aw, Claud, it was a *joke*," said Kristy. "Come on."

"Well, I don't *have* any ideas."

"Okay, okay, we'll keep thinking. Now I'm going to write out our code words. You guys *have* to keep these a secret. Keep the whole page a secret. *Nobody* should know our code. . . . I'm serious now."

"Okay," we agreed.

"Should we stick with what Stacey said?" asked Kristy.

"What did she say? I forget," said Mary Anne.

"She said, *'Have you found my red ribbon?'* "
I replied quickly, glad to be able to answer
something.

"Right," said Kristy. "And that means that
there's some kind of trouble and the baby-
sitter needs the police."

"I think," I said slowly, "that we should
stick with what Stacey said, but that we should
have a few more code words so we can give
more information."

"Yeah. In case there's a burglar listening in
on the phone, the person who gets the phone
call should answer *in code* to let the baby-sitter
know her message was understood and that
the friend knows where she's sitting and everything," added Stacey.

"How about this for the answer?" suggested
Mary Anne. "The person would say, 'No, the
blue one.' It's simple, and it's still in code."

"That's good," said Kristy, but I could see
her shiver at the very thought of a burglar
listening in on her conversation.

"I think we should also have a way to let
someone know whether we're in really *big*
trouble," said Stacey, "like if a burglar is in
the house and we've actually seen him — or
whether we just *think* there's trouble."

"Yeah," I replied. "That's important."

"Okay," said Kristy, "how about this: After

30

the person who gets the call for help goes, 'No, the blue one,' the baby-sitter goes, 'Now I'm in for it,' if there's big trouble, or, 'That's okay,' if she's not sure there's trouble?"

"All right," we agreed.

"I sure hope I can keep all this straight," I said.

"Let's practice," Kristy suggested. "Claudia, let's say you're baby-sitting for David Michael at my house and you hear a noise at the window. What would you do?"

"I'd call Stacey," I said.

"Let's hear your conversation. Remember, you don't know where the burglar is, if there is a burglar, so you have to use the code."

"Okay. . . . Okay, I'd pick up the phone and call Stace— "

"*Ring! Ring! Ring!*" said Kristy, imitating the phone.

Stacey placed an imaginary receiver at her ear. "Hello?"

"Hi, Stace. It's Claud. Did you see my ribbon?"

"No. *Have* you *found* my *red* ribbon?" interrupted Kristy.

"No, I haven't," I said.

"*Claud!* Come on. Do it right."

"I'm trying. . . . Okay. Ring, ring, ring."

"Hello?" said Stacey.

"Hi, it's Claudia. How are you?"

"Not 'How are you'!" cried Kristy. "Get to the point. You're not making a social call. You're scared to death!"

I sighed. "Hi, Stacey. It's me, Claudia. Have you . . . have you *found* my red ribbon?"

Silence. Then Stacey burst out laughing. "I forget what I'm supposed to say!"

Kristy looked ready to kill us. "Claud, call Mary Anne instead."

"Okay, Ring, ring."

"Hello?"

"Hi, Mary Anne. It's Claudia. Have you found my red ribbon?"

"No, I haven't."

"No, the blue one!" shouted Kristy. "Mary Anne, *you* made up this part of the code. You ought to know it."

"I know. I just — I don't know. Start over, Claud."

We practiced a while longer, until we had the code pretty well memorized. Even so, Kristy told us that when we each had a copy of the code words, we should read them over once a day to make sure we didn't forget them. She is so bossy sometimes.

Later, as the girls were getting ready to leave my room, Mary Anne suddenly clapped her hand over her mouth. "Oh, no!" she exclaimed.

"What is it?" I asked.

"I just thought of something. What if my father hears about the Phantom Caller? I bet he won't let me baby-sit anymore."

"But we decided we don't have to worry about the Phantom Caller," I pointed out.

"I know, but if Dad finds out about our code words, forget it. It'll give him something to worry about. I don't think he's thought of robbers and stuff."

"Maybe we should keep *all* this a secret from *all* our parents," said Kristy. "You know how parents are. Mary Anne's right. They're big worry-warts. Let's just go on as if we never thought of any of these things today. Agreed?"

"Agreed!"

The emergency meeting of the Baby-sitters Club was over. But our adventure was just beginning.

CHAPTER 4

There he is! There he is! I told myself excitedly. A Trevor-sighting was always a big event.

I was dodging through the halls of Stoneybrook Middle School trying to remain a safe distance behind Trevor Sandbourne without losing sight of him. It was eight o'clock. The first bell would ring in exactly two minutes.

Trevor came to a sudden stop outside the door to the office of *The Literary Voice.* I stopped, too, and someone ran into me from behind. *Crash!* We fell against some lockers. I turned around. I was face-to-face with Alan Gray.

"Watch where you're going!" I said. I straightened my bow tie with the little scottie dogs on it, and patted my hair to see if any damage had been done. My hair is long and I can do lots of things with it. That day I had fixed it in five slim braids, and looped each one up on my head, holding them in place with beaded barrettes that had sparkly streamers attached to them.

"*Me!* What about you?" said Alan as he straightened his books. Then he stalked off, saying in a soft, singsong voice, "Claud and Trevor sitting in a tree, K–I–S–S–I–N–G."

Oh, he makes me so mad! And how did he know about my crush on Trevor, anyway? Someone must have let the cat out of the bag, and I had a good idea who that someone was.

The bell rang then and I had to run all the way to my homeroom. I sat through the roll call and the morning announcements thinking of Trevor. I had this daydream about us:

Our grade is being taken on a field trip to visit the colonial Bradford Mansion in Wutherby. We're split into groups and Trevor and I are in the same group. After we tour the house, we go out back to the gardens and start wandering through the giant maze made of yew hedges. Trevor and I reach a dead end together and are just about to turn around when we realize it's snowing, even though it's June.

"Hey, what's that?" says Trevor. He points to a little wooden door hidden in the bushes.

"I don't know," I reply. "Let's see. Maybe we can get out of the snow for a while."

We open the door and find ourselves in another world. The snow is gone, and so are the maze, the Bradford Mansion, and the other kids. We're no longer in Wutherby. For all I know, we're not even on Earth. Maybe we're in the fourth dimension. It doesn't matter. Wherever we are, we're alone together. . . .

"Claudia?"

I shook myself awake. Darn. I have never been able to finish that daydream. If my teachers would just leave me alone, I could find out what happens.

"Yes?" I was in math class. It was the third time that morning that I'd started the dream.

"May I have your homework, please?" Our teacher, Mr. Peters, was peering at me with great concern. Most of my teachers look at me that way.

"Oh. Sure." I got my homework paper out of my notebook and placed it on the pile. I knew it was all correct because Janine had been my helper for my weekend homework, and she was a real stickler for the math problems, as you can probably imagine.

"Claudia, Claudia," she was always saying, with as much concern as my teachers. "You're confusing *whole* numbers with *even* numbers. A whole number can be even *or* odd, just as long as it's a negative or positive *integer*."

36

Well, that certainly cleared things up. Why can't Janine talk to me like a normal person? When we were little, she used to be normal. We would play together and have fun. She even seemed to have some sort of an imagination, although that's hard to believe now.

Math class ended and I headed slowly for English. I've been dreading English for the last couple of weeks because of this book we're reading. It's called *The Pond* and I'll be honest with you, I just don't get it. It's not that I don't understand the words; I know all the vocabulary. It's just that I'm not getting much out of it except that this kid goes squirrel-hunting a lot. I'm sure there's more to the story than that — some kind of message — but I don't know what it is. Furthermore, I don't care. Maybe if I didn't try to read it so *fast*. . . .

School is absolutely a complicated mess. Give me Nancy Drew any day.

In English we had to read aloud from *The Pond*. The teacher told me to read with more feeling. Then she handed back these vocabulary quizzes we'd taken the week before. I got a seventy. That was not going to please anybody in my family. It didn't please *me*. I know that you spell *October* O–C–T–O–B–E–R, but I'd written O–C–O–B–E–R. *Pay attention, Claudia.*

I was very glad to get to the cafeteria for lunch.

"Stacey!" I called. I'd spotted her ahead of me in the hot-lunch line. "Save me a seat at our table, okay?"

She nodded.

Ordinarily, I might have tried to sneak in line with her, but she was standing right next to this kid, Alexander Kurtzman, who carries a briefcase and wears a jacket and tie, and *lives* to obey rules. One of his favorites is "No frontsies, no backsies," so there was really no point in trying to butt in.

I looked around the cafeteria and saw Kristy and Mary Anne eating with three other girls — Lauren Hoffman and the Shillaber twins, Mariah and Miranda. The Shillaber twins, who are identical, were dressed alike. I couldn't believe it. They are too old for that, I think. But then, Kristy and her friends *can* be babyish. They had even brought bag lunches that day because the hot lunch was chicken divan, which I admit is on the disgusting side. However, it's embarrassing to bring your lunch to school in seventh grade. For one thing, it gives your locker a permanent bologna odor.

I reminded myself that I needed to have a little talk with Miss Kristy Thomas.

I got my chicken divan and sat down with

Stacey. Pretty soon we were joined by Dorianne Wallingford (talk about romantic names), Emily Bernstein, Howie Johnson, Pete Black, and Rick Chow. We were all eating the chicken divan lunch, and the boys had eight desserts among them. They pack away more food at every meal than a football team does.

"Do you guys think you have enough food?" I asked, as I opened my milk carton and arranged the things on my tray.

"Enough for a food sculpture," replied Pete.

"Oh, no! Not today!" I exclaimed with a giggle. The guys had been bringing toothpicks to school and using their milk cartons and garbage and stuff to make food creations. Once they made Mrs. Pinelli, the music teacher. They gave her noodle hair, grape eyes, and an apple head. We got yelled at for wasting food.

Dorianne ignored the boys. She nibbled at her chicken and looked tragic. She can be very dramatic sometimes.

"What is it?" I asked her finally.

Dorianne sighed loudly. The boys stopped scarfing up their food and looked at her. "We got robbed last night," she said. I dropped my fork with a clatter and almost choked on a mouthful of carrots. "You *did?*"

"Well . . . not *us* exactly."

"Who exactly?"

"Nana and Gramps. And it looks like the work of . . . the Phantom Caller!"

I think my heart actually stopped beating for a few moments.

"The Phantom Caller?" I squeaked.

Dorianne nodded her head tragically.

"Wh–where do your grandparents live?" I asked, dreading her answer.

"In New Hope." Dorianne allowed a tiny bit of chicken to enter her mouth.

I let out a sigh of relief. So the caller was back in New Hope. "Oh, *well*," I said. "In *New Hope*. That's okay."

"Claudia, what are you talking about? He got Nana's sapphire and diamond engagement ring and her diamond choker."

"I'm sorry, Dor," I said. "I didn't mean. . . . It's just that, well, it's better than if he were robbing houses here in Stoneybrook, isn't it?"

Dorianne gave me a funny look. "I guess."

Splat! The boys had lost interest in our conversation and had started a food sculpture. Half a banana had just fallen off a tower of milk cartons and landed in Emily's chicken divan. The chicken splattered onto her mohair sweater.

"Ew, ew!" she cried. "Rick! Look what you did! My sister is going to kill me!"

"Why is your sister going to kill you?" he asked.

"Because this is her sweater."

"Oh. Sorry."

"Come on, Emily," I said "Let's go to the girls' room. I'll help you wash it off."

"All right."

As I stood in the bathroom sponging off Emily's front with damp paper towels, Emily leaned forward and whispered, "So, what is this about you and Trevor Sandbourne?"

My heart stopped beating again. If that kept up, I wouldn't live to see thirteen. I checked in the stalls to make sure we were alone. "Nothing," I said. "And what did you hear?"

"That you like him."

"Who'd you hear it from?"

"Dorianne."

"Who'd she hear it from?"

Emily shrugged. "I don't know."

"Well, I know something. I know that Kristy Thomas has a big, fat mouth."

"Kristy!" exclaimed Emily. "What does she care about stuff like this?"

"She cares." But Emily's words made me think. This *wasn't* the kind of thing Kristy cared about. . . . But she *was* a blabbermouth. I threw away the paper towels. "There," I said to

Emily. "I think the spots are gone."

"Thanks, Claud."

As we walked out into the hall, we ran into Kristy and Mary Anne. "Thanks for nothing!" I said to Kristy.

"What's that supposed to mean?"

Emily raised an eyebrow at us and disappeared into the cafeteria.

"You told about Tr— " I realized I was almost yelling, so I lowered my voice to a whisper. " — about Trevor."

"I did not!" Kristy whispered back.

"Well, everyone seems to know about us. Even Alan Gray."

"Why would *I* speak to *Alan Gray?*" hissed Kristy.

I paused. "Beats me."

"Beats me, too."

Suddenly I felt bad. "I'm sorry, Kristy. I just can't figure out how everyone knows about this."

"Who else did you tell?" asked Mary Anne.

"Just you guys and Stacey."

"Well, *I* didn't say anything."

"And I don't think Stacey would."

"It's a mystery," said Kristy.

"Yeah." A mystery. I liked the sound of that. But I still didn't like everyone knowing my private business. "I'm sorry," I said again.

"Look, I'll see you guys at the meeting this afternoon, okay?" The Baby-sitters Club meets Mondays, Wednesdays, and Fridays from five-thirty to six o'clock to take phone calls from clients.

"Okay." Kristy and Mary Anne disappeared into the girls' room.

I went back to the cafeteria.

Two good things happened that day. The first, of course, had been the Trevor-sighting in the morning. The second happened just before the final bell rang, when Mr. Taylor, the principal, came over the intercom with the afternoon announcements.

He reminded us about having our school pictures taken and about some club meetings. Then he said, "On Friday, October thirty-first — that's Halloween, kids" — duh — "our first school dance, the Halloween Hop, will take place. It will be held in the main gymnasium from four o'clock until six o'clock. Costumes are not required, but they're welcome. We hope to see all of you there. By the way, the dance committee will have a fifteen-minute meeting in my office right after the last bell. That's all. Good afternoon."

I sighed dreamily. The Halloween Hop. Would Trevor go? More important, would he ask me to go? Well, he might — but not if he didn't know who I was. That would be crucial in getting an invitation. I sighed again. The second sigh was hopeless. After all, Trevor didn't even know I was alive.

CHAPTER 5

"Hi-hi!" Jamie Newton flung open his front door and greeted me happily. Jamie is three years old. Kristy and I are his favorite baby-sitters. Jamie is always glad to see us.

"Hi!" I said. "Are you ready to play?"

"Yup!"

Mrs. Newton appeared in the doorway behind Jamie. "Hello, Claudia," she said. "You're right on time." She held the door open for me, and I walked in and followed Mrs. Newton to the kitchen.

Mrs. Newton is one of my favorite people in the whole world. She never asks me about school, but she always asks me about my art and tells me she likes what I'm wearing. Mrs. Newton is pregnant. Jamie is going to have a little brother or sister soon. Very soon. Mrs. Newton is so big she looks as if she should fall over forward instead of standing up straight.

"Oh, Claudia," she said, "what wonderful

barrettes! Where did you get them?"

My barrettes were teddy bears with streamers attached. "At The Merry-Go-Round," I replied. "Three dollars and seventy-five cents."

"Hmm. Maybe I'll get a pair. Not for me, of course. For the baby. I'm sort of hoping for a G–I–R–L."

I smiled.

"I have to spell that," she added, "because Jamie wants a B–O–Y. How are your art classes? What are you working on now?"

"Two oil paintings. We just started using oils. I'm doing a portrait of Mimi and a still life."

"What's in the still life?"

"An egg, a checkered napkin, a wooden spoon, and a pitcher."

"An egg! That must be difficult."

"Yeah, it is. But I like working on it."

Mrs. Newton checked her watch. "I better get going," she said. "I'll be at the doctor's first for a quick checkup, then I just have to stop in at the post office and the grocery store. I'll be home by five o'clock, maybe a bit earlier. You know where the phone numbers are."

"Sure," I said. "Jamie and I are going to have fun. Want to play outside, Jamie?" It was a gray, dreary day, but it wasn't raining.

"Yea!"

I was glad he did, because I was just a little afraid of the Phantom Caller. I knew he usually struck after dark, and I knew he hadn't robbed anyone in Stoneybrook — yet — but I was still scared.

Mrs. Newton left, and I put Jamie's jacket on him. We went into his backyard. The Newton's yard is really good for little kids to play in. There's a slide and a swingset and a jungle gym, and the yard is completely surrounded by a tall stockade fence.

I pushed Jamie on the swing for a while. Then he jumped off and ran to the jungle gym to show me a trick he'd learned. I was facing the house, watching him, when I saw something that nearly made me jump out of my skin.

A light came on downstairs in the Newtons' house. It lit up the living room, but it didn't look like a living room light. Maybe it was in the front hall.

A chill ran up my spine.

I looked at my watch. Four o'clock. Mrs. Newton should have been with the doctor right then. Besides, if she'd come back, I would have heard her car pull up and the door slam.

As I stared at the house, the light went off.

I gasped.

Maybe it was some kind of illusion — like a

street lamp. But why would a street lamp turn on and then go off?

I decided to ignore the light.

Jamie stood up on the bottom of his slide. "Hey, guess who I am!" he yelled. He beat his chest and cried, "Ah! Ah-ah-ah-ah!"

"Peter Rabbit?" I said.

Jamie laughed. "No!"

"Superman?"

"No!"

"Not Tarzan," I said.

"Yes! I'm Tarzan."

At that moment, the phone began to ring. I looked at the house.

"I hear the telephone," said Jamie. "Maybe it's Daddy."

I'd been hoping he wouldn't hear it. I hadn't planned to answer it.

Jamie ran for the house. "Come on!" he said.

I knew I should answer the phone. As a baby-sitter, that was one of my responsibilities. But I was too afraid. I stooped down. "Just a second," I called. "My shoe's untied." I took long enough untying and retying my sneaker so that by the time I caught up with Jamie at the back door, the phone was no longer ringing. "I'm sorry, Jamie," I said. "Look, if it was your dad, he'll call back."

"Okay." Jamie didn't seem too upset. He sat down on the patio and began playing with a dump truck. "Beep, beep! Beep, beep! . . . Hey, what was that?" he asked, holding still.

"What was what?"

"That noise."

"What noise?"

Pat, pat, pat.

"*That* noise."

I had heard it, too. Footsteps on the driveway, on the other side of the stockade fence.

I didn't know what to do. I was afraid to take Jamie into the house, but the only way to leave the Newtons' yard was through the gate in the fence. And the gate opened onto the driveway.

"Maybe it was the paperboy," I suggested.

Jamie shook his head. "The paperboy doesn't come up to our house. He stands in the street and throws the paper into the flower garden."

Pat, pat, pat.

"Hey," I whispered, "let's be spies. Let's sneak up to the fence and peek through the knothole by the gate."

"Okay," Jamie whispered back.

I took Jamie's hand and we tiptoed across the grass to the gate. Very cautiously, I closed one eye and put the other one up to the hole.

A brown eye was looking back at me!

I screamed.

Jamie screamed.

The person attached to the brown eye screamed.

That last scream sounded awfully familiar. "Kristy?" I said.

"Claudia?" The gate opened and Kristy came in, trembling.

"What were you doing?" I shouted.

"Trying to find you," she said. "Hi, Jamie."

"Hi-hi."

"I thought you were the — PC," I said, nodding toward Jamie.

"Sorry. Mom got home from work early today, so I'm off the hook with David Michael." (Kristy and her older brothers each have to take care of their littlest brother, David Michael, one afternoon a week while Mrs. Thomas is at work. A baby-sitter comes on the other days.) "I knew you were baby-sitting here," she went on. "Mom sent me over with something for Mrs. Newton and I wanted to see how you were doing. I was sort of worried about the — PC myself."

"Did you turn on a light in the Newtons' house?"

Kristy nodded. "Mom made a casserole for the Newtons since Mrs. Newton doesn't feel much like cooking anymore. I had to put on a

50

light so I wouldn't trip with it on my way to the refrigerator. Then I went back outside to look for you guys."

"I guess that wasn't you on the phone then," I said.

Kristy's eyes opened wide. "The phone rang?"

"Just a couple of minutes ago, while you were walking around looking for us."

"Did you answer it?"

"No, we — we missed it."

"I bet it was Daddy," said Jamie.

Kristy and I exchanged knowing looks.

"Do you want me to stay for a while?" asked Kristy.

"Yes!" said Jamie and I, for different reasons.

Kristy can be a blabbermouth and a baby, but she can also be a very good friend.

CHAPTER 6

That night, Janine helped me with my homework. She is picky, picky, picky. I bet teachers wouldn't even notice half the things she makes me correct. We were just finishing up when a great crash of thunder sounded.

"Gosh, it's late in the season for thunderstorms," Janine remarked.

"Ooh, but I love them," I said. "They make me feel all shivery. . . . Janine?"

"Hmm?"

"Remember when we were little and we'd crawl under Mom and Dad's bed during thunderstorms? We'd pretend we were camping — "

"But we were really just hiding."

"Yeah," I said fondly.

"Very interesting, psychologically," said Janine. "The fear process — "

"Janine?"

"What?"

"Shut up."

Janine glared at me, then stalked out of the room. I knew Mimi had said I would have to work at being Janine's friend, and she was right. It would take a *lot* of work. How did Janine get the "fear process" out of something as nice as autumn thunderstorms? Even so, I resolved not to give up so easily the next time we talked.

I flicked on the radio and turned it to the local station. I listened to it while I worked on my still life. Maybe the weather report would mention something about the thunderstorm.

I dabbed away at the gray area under the egg. It's hard to figure out what shape shadow an egg will cast.

The music came to an end and I perked up my ears. "At the top of the news," said the radio newscaster suddenly, "is a local story. The thief dubbed the Phantom Caller has been spotted in a stolen car, traveling south through New Jersey. State troopers are tailing him. Details on the hour."

"All right!" I cried. "He's gone!" I was so excited that I turned off the radio, snatched up the phone, and called Stacey. "Guess what! Guess what!" I cried.

"What?" said Stacey excitedly. "Wait. Trevor called you, right? Oh, I knew he would. I *knew* it! Oh, Claud, did he ask — "

"Stacey, Stacey," I said. "That's not it." I felt like a deflated balloon. "He didn't call. It's something else." Unfortunately, the something else wasn't as exciting as Trevor.

"Oh," said Stacey.

"The Phantom Caller's gone. I just heard it on the radio."

"You're kidding."

"Nope. Heading south through New Jersey. Away from us. The police are after him."

"Oh, I hope they catch him."

"Well, even if they don't, he's out of our hair. We can forget about the Phantom Caller for good."

A little while later, I hung up the phone. Then I called Kristy to tell her the news, and then I called Mary Anne.

Boy, were we relieved.

The next evening I had a sitting job for two little girls, Nina and Eleanor Marshall. On school nights I'm allowed to baby-sit until nine-thirty. The deal with my homework is that it must get done in the afternoon. I worked on it with my mother.

At seven-thirty that night, I was in the Marshalls' kitchen, pouring a glass of milk for Nina, who's three. (Eleanor, who's just a year old, was already in bed.) The radio was playing in the background. Nina was watching TV in the den.

Then, just like the night before, a song ended, and the announcer began the evening news with a piece about the Phantom.

Oh, good! I thought. They've captured him.

But I was wrong. Very wrong.

"The man thought to be the Phantom Caller," said the newscaster, "has been captured — and is not the Phantom. The Phantom Caller is still at large."

Still at large! What a horrible way to phrase that. It sounded as if he might be anywhere . . . maybe in the Marshalls' backyard . . . or peering through the kitchen window.

I turned off the radio.

Then I dared to look around to see whether the Phantom Caller was at the window. All I could see were the kitchen lights reflected in the glass.

I put the carton of milk in the refrigerator and picked up the glass. "Nina!" I called. "Here's your milk."

She scurried into the kitchen just as the phone rang. "I want to talk," she said.

I was trembling, but I tried not to let Nina know. "Only if it's your Mom," I told her. I picked her up, and lifted the receiver, dreading the voice I might hear, hoping it really was

Mrs. Marshall just calling to check on things.

"Hello?" I said lightly (for Mrs. Marshall's benefit).

Silence.

"Hello? . . . *Hello?*"

More silence. Then a click as the caller hung up.

Oh, my gosh. The Phantom Caller was in Stoneybrook. I just knew it.

I wondered if I should call Stacey and give her our coded message. What was I supposed to ask about? Barrettes? Ribbons.

"Claudia?"

I jumped a mile as Nina asked, "Who is it?"

"Wrong number," I said. I hung up the phone, put her down, and handed her the milk. "Well, let's go watch TV," I suggested.

"I can't anymore."

"Why not?"

"Because *The Muppet Show* is over. I have to go to bed." Nina was getting a milk mustache.

"So soon?"

"That's my bedtime. After *The Muppet Show.*"

I knew what her bedtime was, but maybe just once she could stay up a little longer. "How about a special treat?" I said excitedly. "You can stay up until eight o'clock."

"But Mommy and Daddy don't let me. That's the rule."

What was I doing, anyway, trying to convince a three-year-old to keep me company? "Okay, then. Upstairs we go."

Nina handed me her empty glass. I put it in the sink and we climbed the stairs. I turned on every light I could possibly find. I wondered what kind of jewelry Mrs. Marshall had.

After Nina was in bed, I tiptoed to Eleanor's room to check on her. I stood in the doorway and let the light from the hall shine into her bedroom. I stared at her crib.

It looked empty!

Oh, my gosh! Maybe the Phantom Caller was in the Marshalls' house somewhere and he'd taken Eleanor! I dashed over to her crib. There she was, all bunched into a corner. I straightened her out and covered her up again.

Eleanor sighed in her sleep.

I sighed, too.

I turned off the upstairs lights and went back down to the den. I turned the TV on. Then I turned it off. If the TV was on, the Phantom Caller could sneak up on me too easily. I sat in the silence and flipped through a magazine.

Crick, crick, crick.

What was that?

Just the Marshalls' cat settling down on a pile of newspapers.

Plink, plink.

What was that?

Water dripping in the sink.

All the little noises were driving me crazy. I put the TV back on. I tried to watch it, but my gaze kept traveling to the dark windows that faced the backyard. Finally, I couldn't stand it any longer. I shut the curtains.

Then I decided to call Stacey.

"Claudia!" Stacey exclaimed when she got on the phone. "Have you been listening to the news?"

"Yes!" I said. "What do you think?"

"I was just going to call you because I know you're baby-sitting. I don't know *what* to think!"

"Oh, it's so spooky here. Every little noise makes me jump. And you know what? The phone rang a while ago, and *the caller didn't say a word.* He just hung up."

"Oooh. But you're . . . you're not asking about your hair ribbons," Stacey said cautiously.

"No," I replied. "Not yet."

"Do you want me to come over?"

"I do, but I don't want the Marshalls to come home and find you here with me. I don't want them to think I can't handle a simple job by myself."

"Well, do you want to stay on the phone awhile?"

"Yes. That would be great." I decided I didn't care whether Mrs. Marshall was trying to call.

"So what's going on with Trevor?" asked Stacey.

"Oh, the usual."

"Nothing?"

"Yeah. I wonder if he even knows about the Halloween Hop. Poets are sometimes off in their own worlds. Maybe he hasn't heard the announcements in school."

"Oh, I bet he has," said Stace. "How could anyone miss them?" She put her hand over the receiver to disguise her voice and did a pretty good imitation of Mr. Taylor talking on the intercom. "As you know, children, Halloween falls on October thirty-first this year."

I giggled. "Taylor is so dumb. He thinks we — " I broke off.

"Claudia?" asked Stacey.

"Shh." I held the phone away from my ear and listened intently. I definitely heard footsteps in the garage. "Stacey, Stacey," I said urgently. "Have you found my b— I mean, did you see my — Have you found my . . . my. . . ."

"Your red ribbon?" whispered Stacey.

"Yes!" I gasped.

"Yes, I did. I mean, no, I found — I. . . ."

59

"Did you find my blue — Oh, no, Stacey, someone's at the garage door. I can hear the knob rattling!"

"I'm going to call the police."

"Claudia?" called a deep voice.

It was all I could do not to shriek. "He called my name!" I yelped to Stacey.

"Claudia," said the voice again, "we've misplaced the house keys. Can you let us in, please?"

I let my breath out in one long, shaking sigh. "It's the Marshalls, Stace," I whispered. "Gotta go. I'll call you when I get home."

I ran to the back door, unlocked it, and flung it open. I have never, ever, in my whole life, been so glad to see anybody.

"Hi, Claudia," said Mrs. Marshall.

Mr. Marshall was standing behind her, patting his pockets, and muttering, "I can't figure out where those darned keys went."

I held the door open for them. "Sorry for the confusion," Mrs. Marshall went on. "The house keys may be at Mr. Marshall's office. Here, dear, use mine," said Mrs. Marshall to her husband. She took a ring of keys from a peg in the back hall and handed it to him. Then she turned to me. "How were the girls tonight?"

"Oh, just fine," I said. "Nina went to bed

as soon as *The Muppet Show* was over."

"Good. No problems, then?"

"None at all." I was still shaking.

Mrs. Marshall began rummaging through her purse for money.

A few minutes later, as Mr. Marshall was opening the door to walk me home, the phone rang. I heard Mrs. Marshall pick it up and say hello. Then I heard her hang up, saying, "That's strange."

I shivered. It was strange all right.

CHAPTER 7

Thursday, October 23

This evening I baby-sat at Watson's. It's hard to believe Watson will become my stepfather next year. Oh, well.

As I promised the rest of the club members last Saturday, I've been bringing our club record book to school every day so each of us can check the appointments and see where the others will be baby-sitting. After tonight, I'm not so sure that's a good idea. See, Karen, Watson's five-year-old daughter, was so nervous about the woman next door who she thinks is a witch, that she was making me nervous. Then, just when I was about the most scared I've ever been, the phone started ringing... and ringing... and ringing...

Poor Kristy. I'm glad she and Watson, her mother's boyfriend, finally get along better. But I guess it is a little frightening to sit at his house. I've never done it, but Mary Anne has. She was spooked, too. And that was a while ago, before we knew anything about the Phantom Caller. For starters, Watson's house is huge, practically a mansion, and the house next door, which is also huge, is gloomy and rambling, with turrets and towers and dark windows everywhere. If that weren't bad enough, little Karen is convinced that Mrs. Porter, who lives there, is a witch named Morbidda Destiny who has put two spells on Boo-Boo, Watson's fat cat. On the night Kristy was baby-sitting, Karen had a new twist on her fears about Mrs. Porter.

Kristy arrived at Watson's at seven. She can't baby-sit very late on week nights, but Watson was only going to Parents' Night at Karen's private school, so he was going to be home early. Usually his kids, Karen and Andrew, don't stay with him during the week, but since his ex-wife had broken her ankle, Watson was taking them more often than usual.

"Hi, Kristy!" Karen cried, when Mrs. Thomas dropped Kristy off at Watson's.

"Hi!" added Andrew happily. Andrew is three.

Andrew and Karen like Kristy so much that not long ago, Kristy promised them she'd be their main baby-sitter at Watson's until she becomes their stepsister.

Watson walked into the front hall. "Well, Kristy," he said warmly, "I'm so glad you could come." (Kristy knew that Watson was really just glad she wasn't such a pill about him and her mother anymore.) "I don't think you'll have any trouble tonight."

Kristy smiled at Watson as Boo-Boo wandered into the hall. "I know one way to avoid trouble," she said. "We'll keep Boo-Boo inside." She turned to Karen and grinned at her, but Karen just stared back solemnly. Uh-oh, thought Kristy. Something's wrong.

"All right," said Watson, "the emergency numbers are in the usual place, and the phone number of Karen's school, plus her classroom number, are taped to the phone, just in case." Kristy nodded. "Seven-thirty-bedtime for Andrew," Watson went on, "and eight o'clock for Karen. By the way, there's peppermint-stick ice cream in the freezer and . . . I don't believe Andrew and Karen have had dessert yet."

"Yea! Ice cream!" cried Andrew, jumping up and down.

Karen continued to look solemn.

64

Kristy began to feel suspicious — and a little nervous.

Watson shrugged into his coat. "Good-bye, pumpkin," he said, kissing the top of Karen's head. "Good-bye, Andy."

He left quickly, calling over his shoulder, "I'll be home before nine, Kristy. Thanks again."

Kristy glanced warily at Andrew and Karen. This was the moment when even the most baby-sat-for children sometimes burst into tears. Jamie Newton, for instance, absolutely hated for his parents to leave him just before bedtime. But Andrew was already on his way into the kitchen after the ice cream. Karen, apparently, had other things on her mind.

"What's the matter?" Kristy finally asked her, taking her hand. She really didn't want to know, yet it was her job to know.

"Morbidda Destiny," whispered Karen.

"What about her?" Kristy whispered back, a little shivery tickle running up her spine. She remembered how strange Mary Anne said Boo-Boo had acted the day she was baby-sitting, when Mrs. Porter had chased him out of her garden with a rake.

"Kristy? Ice cream?" called Andrew from the kitchen.

"Just a sec, Andrew."

"More spells," whispered Karen urgently.

"Really?" asked Kristy, trying to sound unconcerned. "Boo-Boo looks all right."

"Not Boo-Boo. Me," said Karen. She closed her eyes dramatically.

"You!" exclaimed Kristy. "What's she done to you?"

"Given me freckles."

"Karen," said Kristy, hiding a smile, "you already had freckles. You've had freckles since you were two years old. I've seen pictures."

"She's given me more."

"Sometimes they spread."

Karen shook her head.

"Kristy!" called Andrew, sounding impatient.

"Coming! Karen, I really don't think you need to worry. Let's go have some ice cream with Andrew, okay?"

"Okay . . . but I'm warning you. If she squints her eyes and holds one hand in the air, she's putting a spell on you."

"I'll be on the alert," Kristy said.

They walked into the kitchen — and found pink ice cream dripping all over the table and onto the floor. Three bowls and three spoons were sitting stickily in the middle of the mess.

"Andrew!" cried Kristy.

"I helped," he said proudly. "I let Boo-Boo out, too."

66

Kristy turned pale. "You — you let *Boo-Boo* out? Andrew, I — "

"I guess he wasn't paying attention," said Karen quickly.

Kristy calmed down. "I guess not. . . . Andrew, thank you very much for helping. But from now on, maybe you should tell me before you help with Boo-Boo, okay? Sometimes we don't let him outside."

Andrew's face fell.

"But," Kristy rushed on, "you did a good job with the ice cream. Thank you. Let's just wipe up the drips and then we can eat."

Kristy, Karen, and Andrew finished their ice cream. Then Kristy put Andrew to bed and helped Karen change into her pajamas.

"Let's read stories until my bedtime," Karen suggested.

"Okay," said Kristy. "You choose."

Karen searched through the shelf in her room, then sat down on her bed. Kristy sat next to her. Karen handed her a book.

"What's this?" exclaimed Kristy. *"The Witch Next Door?* Where did this come from?"

"It just appeared," said Karen mysteriously.

Kristy looked at her suspiciously. "Are you sure?"

"Well . . . it appeared from inside Daddy's briefcase. He bought it for me."

"Aha!" said Kristy. "Listen, tonight we're going to read something funny." She took a fat book from the shelf. "Has your daddy read this to you?"

Karen shook her head. "It's too long."

"Not if you read it a little at a time, and that's what we're going to do. Every time I baby-sit, we'll read some more."

"Okay," agreed Karen. She settled herself against her pillow.

"Now," said Kristy, "this story is all about a girl exactly your age whose name is Ramona Quimby."

"Goody," said Karen. "I like that name."

Kristy began to read. A half an hour later, Karen was asleep. Kristy tiptoed downstairs. As soon as she reached the kitchen, the phone rang. Kristy practically jumped out of her skin.

The caller was Mary Anne. "Just checking," she said. "I wanted to see how you're doing."

"Fine," Kristy replied. "Karen and Andrew are in bed. But Karen thinks Mrs. Porter has put a freckle-spell on her." Kristy giggled nervously.

"You know," said Mary Anne, "I'd be able to laugh, too, if only Mrs. Porter didn't look so . . . so. . . . "

"So much like a witch?"

"Well, yes. I mean, she goes flapping around her yard in those horrible black robes like some kind of overgrown bat — "

"Mary Anne, stop!"

"Okay. I'm sorry. Look, I'm not supposed to be on the phone at all. I had to tell Dad this was a homework emergency. I'm glad everything's okay."

"Thanks."

"Lock up tight."

"What?"

"The windows. The doors. Lock them. Lock everything — just in case."

"All right."

Kristy and Mary Anne hung up and Kristy started walking through Watson's huge, silent house. All the windows seemed to be locked, but Kristy checked each one anyway. The only problem was that there were so many of them. And the locks on some were hard to reach. Kristy was perched precariously on top of a stepladder in the library when the phone rang again.

"Aughh!" Kristy stumbled down the ladder. She reached for the phone on the big leather desk. Then she drew her hand back, afraid. After three rings, she told herself it was probably just Mary Anne calling back, even though she knew that was unlikely. Mr. Spier is *so* strict about letting his daughter talk on the phone after dinner.

"Hello?" said Kristy timidly. ". . . Hello?"

She thought she could hear light breathing on the other end of the phone.

"Hello?" Nothing. Kristy dropped the receiver into the cradle as if it were burning her hand. She ran from the library. She knew she should check the upstairs windows, but she was too afraid. I just know the Phantom Caller is going to sneak onto the second floor, she told herself. He's probably leaning a ladder against the outside of the house at this very moment. He's —

Ring! The phone again.

Ring. . . . Ring.

At last Kristy reached for it. She knew she had to answer it. The caller could be Watson or her mother. She picked up the receiver and held it to her ear. But she couldn't get any words out.

"Kristy?" asked the caller.

"Claudia?" she whispered back. (The caller was me!)

"What's wrong?" I asked her.

"I just got one of those calls."

"Oooh."

"And Watson's house is so huge and scary."

"Put on lots of lights," I suggested.

"What do you think the calls mean?" Kristy asked. She couldn't stop thinking about them. I knew just how she felt.

"Well," I said, "they could be wrong numbers. People are pretty rude when they reach the wrong person. They usually just hang up. Or they could be little kids making goof calls."

"I guess," said Kristy.

"In case there's any trouble, do you remember our code?"

"No."

"Kristy! You were the one who made us rehearse. Where's your sheet with the code words?"

"At home. I didn't know how it would feel to be so nervous. I can't even remember my last name."

"It's Thomas."

"Thanks a lot."

"Kristy. You are the baby-sitter. You're in charge. You better act like it."

Silence. Then, "You're right. Okay, Claud, I'm going to get off this phone and go read *The Witch of Blackbird Pond*."

"Are you sure you want to read *that*?"

"I have to. It's for school. Besides, there are no such things as witches, and I'm through being scared. I'm a baby-sitter."

"Right."

"Right."

"See you in school tomorrow."

"Right. Good-bye." Kristy hung up brusquely. She marched out of the library, got her book, and curled up with it on the living room couch. But she couldn't concentrate. She kept looking outside. The branches of the trees in Watson's yard moved eerily back and forth in front of the street lamps. They looked sort of like hands — gloved hands.

One little branch kept tap-tapping on the bay window right by Kristy's head. Tap-tap. Tap-tap.

Kristy could imagine all sorts of Halloweeny creatures in Watson's yard. Cackling witches, howling goblins, silent, watching ghouls.

Tap-tap. Tap-tap.

Then Kristy heard another sound. Or thought she did. A sort of swooshing. It was followed by an angry yowl at the front door. "Boo-Boo!" cried Kristy. She was glad he was coming in on his own. She could stop worrying about Mrs. Porter and her garden.

Kristy ran into the front hall and flung the door open.

There was Boo-Boo all right. But he wasn't alone. He was in the black-clothed arms of . . . Morbidda Destiny!

It was the first time Kristy had actually seen her, although she had imagined her vividly after Mary Anne's encounter. No wonder Karen thought she was a witch. An old, whiskery face with snappish little eyes sat under a mop of frowsy gray hair. And sure enough, she was wearing a long, black dress. Watson said Mrs. Porter was just eccentric, but Kristy was not at all sure.

She gasped when she saw her.

"This cat," said Morbidda Destiny, "was on my front porch."

"I — I'm sorry," said Kristy. "He got out by accident. I hope he wasn't bothering you."

Morbidda Destiny deposited Boo-Boo in an ungraceful heap in Watson's front hall. Boo-Boo tore out of the hall, heading for the laundry room.

"Wasn't *bothering* me?" cried Morbidda Destiny. "Do you know what he was *doing* on my porch, girlie?"

Kristy shook her head.

"He was eating a field mouse, that's what. And do you know what's left on my porch now?"

Kristy shook her head again, shuddering.

"A bit of fur, a bit of tail, and — "

"I'm so sorry, Mor— Mrs. Porter," Kristy interrupted. "I'd like to come over and clean it up, but I'm baby-sitting here and I can't leave the — "

"Never you mind. I've taken care of it." Morbidda Destiny reached into her robes, pulled out a small paper bag, and thrust it at Kristy. "These are the remains. You get rid of them."

She turned and flapped into the night.

Now I'll prove to you just how smart Kristy is. Kristy said that right then, when Mrs. Porter shoved that bag into her hands, she was really scared. And she was really disgusted by what was in the bag. But you know what her first thought was? It was that if Mrs. Porter were a true witch, she would have kept the bag for herself because she could have used the mouse fur and mouse tail in her spells. So even though Kristy was shaking all over, she was relieved, too.

She checked on Boo-Boo and found him curled up in a laundry basket in front of the washing machine. He wasn't asleep — he was just resting and staring — which was a little creepy, but he seemed fine.

When Watson got home, Kristy told him about Boo-Boo and the field mouse and the paper bag. Watson said he would speak to Mrs. Porter the next morning. Then Kristy told him about Karen and the freckle-spell.

"I can't tell whether she believes in the spell

or whether it's all a big game, but I thought you should know," she said.

"Thank you, Kristy. I appreciate your concern. It seems that she's been talking about witches at school, too."

"Well, I better call Mom," said Kristy.

She had to wait fifteen minutes for her mother to pick her up, and even though Watson was there with her, Kristy said that the whole time she kept waiting for the phone to ring again.

CHAPTER 8

Saturday, October 25th

Last night I sat for Charlotte Johanssen. She's a nice little kid, an only child, and absolutely no problem. In fact, she's kind of timid and shy, which bothers me sometimes. It makes me feel like I have to be brave and protective when I'm around her. And sometimes I don't feel brave at all. Like last night. I was already worried about the Phantom and phone calls. I mean, after the experiences Kristy and Claudia have had, who wouldn't be? So when the storm came, I nearly fell apart. Luckily, though, I'm a good baby-sitter, and when you're a good baby-sitter, baby-sitting comes first. So somehow, I managed to keep my head.

Hmphh. If that's what Stacey calls keeping her head, I wouldn't want to see her lose it.

Stacey left for the Johanssens' after an early supper. She was going to be sitting until ten, the latest she's allowed out. If you cut through Stacey's backyard and turn right, the Johanssens' house is just two doors down — a three-minute walk. If you use the streets and go around the long way, it takes about ten minutes. Stacey used the shortcut, even though the night seemed darker than usual and she had to carry a flashlight.

Mr. Johanssen met her at the front door. (His wife is hardly ever around. She's a doctor and spends a lot of time at Stoneybrook General Hospital.) "Hi, Stacey," he greeted her. "I'm glad you could come. I'll be meeting Dr. Johanssen at the theater. The number is there by the phone. We're going to see an early movie and then have a bite to eat at Renwick's. That number is posted, too. I know you need to be home by ten.

"Charlotte has finished her dinner and ought to be in bed by nine-thirty, okay?"

Stacey nodded.

"I guess you know everything else."

Stacey nodded again, and smiled as Charlotte came into the kitchen. "Charlotte and I will have lots of fun, won't we?"

"Yes," replied Charlotte uncertainly. "Daddy, do you have to go?"

Mr. Johanssen put his arm around Charlotte. "Mommy and I have been looking forward to this movie. It's a treat for us. But you'll have a treat when you wake up tomorrow."

"What?" asked Charlotte excitedly.

"Mommy will be here, and she's not working this weekend."

"Goody!"

Now, all the time Stacey and Charlotte and Mr. Johanssen were talking, Stacey had been noticing something. If the evening had seemed dark on her way over to the Johanssens', it was positively black just ten minutes later. And it was only six-thirty. It seemed rather windy, too. The branches of the trees, already half bare, were being tossed back and forth. Stacey thought she heard thunder in the distance, but she tried not to worry about it. We'd had a lot of late-season storms, and most of them didn't last long.

Mr. Johanssen left a few moments later, taking an umbrella with him. Stacey and Charlotte stood at the front window and watched his car back slowly down the driveway and turn onto the street. Just as the headlights disappeared from view, the rain started. It came pouring down, as if someone had overturned a huge pail of water in the sky.

"Close all the windows!" cried Charlotte.

"Turn on the lights!" cried Stacey, already spooked.

Stacey and Charlotte ran through the house, closing windows (there weren't many open) and turning on lights.

"What do you want to do now?" asked Stacey, when they were finished.

"Watch TV," replied Charlotte.

Crash! A huge clap of thunder sounded, and Charlotte raced to Stacey's side. "I *hate* thunder," she confessed.

"You, too?" asked Stacey. "You know what I used to do during a thunderstorm?"

"What?"

"Hide in the linen closet. It was the smallest closet in our apartment in New York City. I'd run in, slide under the bottom shelf, and close the door after me, pulling it from the bottom. Sometimes I'd take my Raggedy Andy with me."

Charlotte giggled. "Once," she said, "I hid under my bed during a storm. The storm lasted so long I fell asleep and Mommy and Daddy didn't know where I was. They almost called the police!"

Crash! Ba-room! More thunder. Lightning flashed and zigzagged through the sky.

"Quick, let's put on the TV," said Stacey.

She and Charlotte ran into the family room. Charlotte flicked on the TV, and Stacey found the remote control unit. They started switching from channel to channel. They found an interview, a cooking show, and two news programs.

"Boring," said Stacey. "Let's put on MTV. At least we could hear some good music."

"What's MTV?" asked Charlotte.

"Music television. Where's your cable box?"

"We don't have cable," said Charlotte. "Not yet. Daddy said maybe this winter."

"Rats," said Stacey. She went back to the remote control.

Flick, flick, flick. They looked at all the regular channels and even tried to tune in some of the UHF stations.

"Boring, boring, boring," said Stacey.

"Double rats," said Charlotte.

"Hey," said Stacey. "Here's something." She had tuned into Channel 47. A large, ghostly hand was walking around in a cemetery all by itself. At the top of the screen were the words SPOOK THEATRE and under them, WATCH AT YOUR OWN RISK.

"Ooh, spooky!" said Charlotte. She edged closer to Stacey on the couch.

"Shall we try it?" asked Stacey. "It's better

80

than anything else that's on."

"Okay," agreed Charlotte.

Stacey and Charlotte watched a commercial that showed a can of cleanser dancing around a bathroom. Then SPOOK THEATRE appeared on the screen again, and finally the movie began. It started with a nighttime shot of a huge, gloomy mansion sitting alone on a rise of land. Lightning flashed and thunder rumbled.

"Kind of like our weather," Charlotte remarked, as a clap of real thunder sounded, followed by a streak of lightning. The lamps flickered.

Charlotte moved as close to Stacey as she could get without sitting in her lap. Stacey put her arm around her. They looked at each other and giggled.

"I have goose bumps!" exclaimed Charlotte.

On the television, the scene changed to a bedroom inside the mansion. It was lit only by two candles. A young woman with long, dark hair glided into the room. She was wearing a white dressing gown and carrying another candle.

She walked across the room to a set of French doors that opened onto a balcony, and began to close them, the wind from the storm making her gown billow softly around her. Just when she had almost pulled the doors closed, she gasped and let out a small cry.

"What?" whispered Charlotte.

On the lawn below the woman, Stacey and Charlotte could make out a dark figure.

"Lenora," wailed the figure, "I've come back. Back from beyond the grave."

Lenora moaned and dropped her candle. Thunder crashed. Then thunder from the real storm outside crashed even more loudly. For a moment, the room Stacey and Charlotte were in seemed to glow brightly. A second later, it was plunged into darkness.

The girls screamed. Charlotte clutched Stacey. Everything had gone off — the lights, the TV, all the electricity. It was so quiet they could hear their own hearts pounding. But worse than the silence was the utter blackness.

"Power failure," whispered Stacey.

"I want my mommy," murmured Charlotte. "Or my daddy."

Stacey tried to pull herself together. "There's really nothing to be afraid of," she told Charlotte. "So the electricity went off. So what? The pilgrims lived their whole lives without electricity. You should be in New York when there's a power failure. The entire city practically stops running. We lived on the seventeenth floor of an apartment building and when the power went out, so did the elevators.

Imagine having to walk up seventeen flights of stairs just to get home."

"Yuck," said Charlotte.

"I'll say. Now," Stacey went on, feeling a bit better, "what we have to do is get some candles."

"Like Lenora's?" asked Charlotte.

"Well, yes. Where do your parents keep them?"

"I don't know. I'm not allowed to light matches."

"Don't you have any idea?"

"Maybe in the chest of drawers in the dining room."

"Good. All right, now we'll just find my flashlight and we can use it to light our way into the dining room."

Stacey stood up, holding tightly to Charlotte's hand. They began edging toward the front hall where Stacey had left her jacket and the flashlight.

Shuffle, shuffle, shuffle, *crash!*

"Ow!" yelled Stacey.

"What?"

"My toe. I walked right into something." Stacey felt around. "A table, I think. Okay, let's keep going."

Shuffle, shuffle, shuffle.

"Stacey?"

"What, Charlotte?"

Shuffle, shuffle, shuffle.

"I hear something."

"What?"

"I don't know."

Shuffle, shuffle, shuffle.

"There it is again. Stop moving."

Stacey and Charlotte paused, holding their breaths and listening.

And then Stacey heard it — a creak.

"Where's it coming from?" she asked.

"Sounds like the basement," whispered Charlotte.

"Well, let's make sure the door to the basement is closed. Where *is* the door to the basement?"

"Right here." Charlotte moved past Stacey, running her hand along the wall. "Yup, it's closed."

"Okay. Good. Be quiet for a sec."

The girls stopped and listened again.

Creak. Creak, squish, creak, squish, creak, squish.

In the dark, Charlotte's hand found Stacey's. She held on tight.

Creak, squish, creak, squish.

"Something's coming up the stairs!" cried Charlotte softly.

"Shh," was all Stacey said, but she told me

later that what she was thinking was, Ohmi-
gosh! It's the Phantom. He turned off the
electricity to distract us, and now he's sneaking
into the Johanssens' house through the basement!

Creak, squish. The sound was closer. It had
almost reached the top of the stairs.

Stacey was just about to tell Charlotte to
start heading for the back door, when the
creaking stopped. It was followed by a *woof!*

Stacey jumped about a foot, but Charlotte
exclaimed, "Carrot! Oh, it's just Carrot! He
must have come in through the basement
again. There's a broken window down there."

"Who's Carrot?"

"Our schnauzer. He must be sopping. I'll
try to find a towel so we can dry him off."

And at that moment the lights came back
on. Stacey and Charlotte looked at each other
and began to giggle. Then they did dry off the
poor, rain-drenched Carrot, and they even
watched some more of *Spook Theatre.*

Outside the storm died down, and the rest
of the evening was peaceful.

The phone didn't ring once while Stacey was
at the Johanssens'.

CHAPTER 9

Saturday, October 25

   This evening I baby-sat for David Michael. The rest of the Thomases went out for dinner with Watson and Karen and Andrew, but David Michael had to stay at home in bed because he's got a cold.

   I like baby-sitting for David Michael. He's almost like my brother. I've known him since he was born. And he's usually pretty good. But tonight, since he's sick, he fell asleep very early, and I felt all alone. I couldn't think of anything except prowlers and weird phone calls and especially the Phantom. The weather was fine — a little breezy, but not stormy — and there were

Spooked isn't the word. Mary Anne was practically out of her mind. She was just sitting quietly on the couch watching an old *I Love Lucy* show, when suddenly she got goose pimples all along her arms. She jumped up, turned down the volume on the TV, and listened. Nothing. Not a thing. Even so, she dashed upstairs to check on David Michael. He was lying on his side, breathing noisily, a box of Kleenex next to him. Mary Anne left the hall light on and went back downstairs.

She closed every open closet door and turned on two more lights. Then she closed off the laundry room, in case someone was hiding in there. Finally she pulled down the venetian blinds in the den. But still she didn't feel safe, even though Louie, the Thomases' dog, was in the house with her.

What if someone sneaks inside while I'm watching TV? she thought. That was when she decided to rig up the burglar alarms. All three of them.

Now, the thing about Mary Anne Spier is that she may be quiet, and she may be shy, but she *does* have a good sense of humor and a good imagination. You'd have to, to think up the alarms that Mary Anne rigged in the Thomases' house.

Well, actually, the first one wasn't much in terms of imagination. It was the alarm Mary Anne had described at our emergency club meeting the week before: a big stack of pots, pans, and cans from the kitchen built up against the inside of the door into the garage. If anyone tried to get in from the garage, the door would push the stack over and it would crash down, alerting Mary Anne, who would be able to escape out another door and call the police. The burglar might even be so startled that he'd turn around and leave.

Mary Anne finished her alarm, sat down in front of the TV again, and immediately decided she ought to rig up the front door, too. She was pretty sure a prowler wouldn't come right through the front door, but you can never tell with prowlers. She was out of pots, pans, and cans, though, so she had to think of something else. She looked at a shelf full of David Michael's toys and her eyes fell on a large bag of marbles.

"*Aha!*" she said aloud.

Mary Anne took the marbles into the front hall. Then she found a long piece of string. She placed the bag of marbles on a table next to the door and attached the string to a little hole near the opening of the bag. She tied the other end securely to the doorknob. This was Mary Anne's idea: The prowler quietly opens the door; the string pulls the marbles to the floor; they spill everywhere, not only making a racket to alert Mary Anne, but causing the prowler to slip and fall when he steps inside.

Naturally, as soon as Mary Anne finished her second alarm, she decided she needed one for the back door. It was the only way she would feel safe. Then she would have all the doors covered.

Mary Anne had to think awhile before making that last alarm. By then, she was out of marbles as well as pots and pans.

What else could make a lot of noise? Mary Anne thought.

Blocks? Maybe.

Tinker toys? Nah.

Music! Music could be good and loud. The plans for Mary Anne's final alarm began to take shape.

First she tiptoed upstairs to Kristy's room to borrow her portable tape deck. Then she looked through the tape collection in the room Sam and Charlie share. She selected one called "Poundin' Down the Walls" by the Slime Kings and slipped it into the tape deck.

Back downstairs she sat on the rug in the den to think, the tape deck in her lap. How could she arrange for the tape deck to turn itself on?

She thought some more. How did *she* turn it on? She pressed the play button, of course. Okay. How could she get something else to press the play button? Better yet, how could she get the back door to press the play button?

In a flash of brilliance, she had the answer. Mary Anne leaped up and carried the tape deck into the kitchen. She sat down on the floor again and examined the skinny, rubber-tipped doorstop attached to the bottom of the back door. Perfect.

Mary Anne set the tape deck about two feet from the door. She lined the doorstop up with the play button. Then she opened the door. The doorstop hit the tape deck and the tape deck fell over. But that didn't stop Mary Anne. I need to . . . to shore it up or something, she thought.

She dragged a heavy, round footstool in from the den and set it just behind the tape deck.

She opened the door again.

The doorstop hit the play button, and "Poundin' Down the Walls" blared out of the tape deck. Mary Anne smiled. Satisfied, she hit the stop button, turned the volume up to ten, and went back into the den. She curled up on the couch with her tattered copy of *The Secret Garden* and began to read.

She was in the middle of one of her favorite parts — the part where Mary discovers poor, sickly Colin hidden in Misselthwaite Manor — when she heard an ominous creak from the front hall. Actually, Mary Anne told me the next day, it was just a little creak, but her head was filled with the dark, shadowy hallways of Misselthwaite, so almost any noise would have sounded ominous.

Mary Anne looked up sharply. She jumped to her feet. "Louie!" she whispered urgently. Where is that dog when you need protection? she asked herself. She tiptoed to the den door and peeped into the hall.

There was Louie. He was standing at attention, staring at the front door.

The hinges creaked slightly.

Louie whined.

And all of a sudden the door flew open, pulling the marbles to the floor and scattering them loudly.

Louie barked twice.

But no one came in.

Mary Anne let out a sigh of relief. "It's just the wind, Louie," she said shakily, "like the wind off the moors in Yorkshire," she added, thinking of her book. "I must not have closed the door all the way."

But Louie didn't look convinced. He sat at the screen door, silently begging to be let out to patrol the property. Mary Anne opened it for him, and then set to work gathering up the marbles. She put them back in the bag, but decided not to rig the alarm again. She settled for locking the screen door, and double-locking the inside door.

Then she returned to *The Secret Garden*. In the story, Mary was having her first conversation with Colin. Suddenly, Mary Anne heard a soft thud.

And then — to her absolute horror —

"Poundin' Down the Walls" blasted on in the kitchen!

Mary Anne let out a bloodcurdling scream as she gazed at the partly open back door. She was just about to make a dash for the front door, when Louie strolled into the kitchen, sniffed curiously at the tape deck, and headed for his water bowl.

"Louie!" exclaimed Mary Anne in a half gasp, half shriek.

She'd forgotten that David Michael had taught Louie how to throw his weight against doors. If they weren't latched properly, they opened, which was occasionally useful to Louie. Mary Anne probably hadn't closed the back door tightly after she'd tested the tape deck alarm.

"Some baby-sitter I am," she scolded herself, "leaving doors open right and left for anybody to walk through."

"Bary Add!" called a voice.

Mary Anne looked around to see David Michael standing sleepily on the stairs, his old stuffed dog in one hand.

"Bary Add, cad you put the busic off?" he asked. "I do't like it. It's too loud." He blinked in the bright light of the hall.

"Oh, my gosh! I'm sorry, David Michael," cried Mary Anne. "I didn't mean to wake you up. Really."

She dashed to the tape deck and turned it off. "That was an accident. I'm sorry. . . . How are you feeling?"

"Stuffy. Ad by head hurts."

"Oh," said Mary Anne sympathetically. She remembered that Mrs. Thomas had said David Michael could have half a children's aspirin if he needed it. "Do you want some aspirin?" she asked him. "It'll make your head feel better."

"Okay," said David Michael wheezily.

"You go back to bed and I'll be right up."

Mary Anne felt better since the house wasn't

so quiet. She brought David Michael the aspirin, and then she sat on his bed and told him a story about a tiny man named Mr. Piebell who lived in the woods on the twelfth floor of an oak tree apartment building with his miniature collie, Louie.

David Michael fell asleep with a smile on his lips.

Mary Anne was just closing the door to his room when she heard a tremendous crash downstairs.

The tin-can burglar alarm! It had gone off and Mary Anne was trapped upstairs where there was no escape route! Heart pounding, she tried to figure out what to do. Should she wake David Michael and bring him into Mrs. Thomas' room while she called the police? Should she risk everything and make a dash for the front door? What if it was just Louie fooling around? Maybe she should call Stacey and try out our code. If only she could remember it. . . .

"Mary Anne?" said an uncertain voice from downstairs.

Yikes! It was a *man's* voice!

Mary Anne shrank into a corner of the hallway.

"Mary Anne?" it called again more loudly.

The voice sounded vaguely familiar. How does the Phantom know my name? wondered Mary Anne.

Then she heard another voice call her. It was Kristy.

Mary Anne dared to peep downstairs. Kristy, Sam, Charlie, Mrs. Thomas, Watson, Karen, and Andrew were standing in a group at the bottom of the stairs looking up at her.

"Oh," said Mary Anne, trying to sound nonchalant, and realizing that the first voice had been Watson's. "I thought I heard you. I just gave David Michael some aspirin and got him back to sleep. He woke up with a headache." She trotted down the stairs.

"Um . . . Mary Anne . . . if you don't mind my asking," said Mrs. Thomas, "what are all those cans and things doing by the door?"

"Oh, *those?*" replied Mary Anne. "Those are just . . . just. . . . Actually, they were sort of a burglar alarm. I meant to put them away before you got home."

Kristy began to giggle. Charlie snorted.

"And my tape deck?" asked Kristy.

Mary Anne demonstrated the back-door alarm, this time with the volume turned down.

"Ingenious," commented Watson.

"It certainly looks as if David Michael is safe

with you," said Mrs. Thomas.

Mary Anne nodded. She knew she was blushing furiously.

"You could start another business of your own," said Sam. "Mary Anne's Surefire Alarm Systems."

Mary Anne blushed even more furiously.

"Come on," said Kristy, after Mrs. Thomas had paid Mary Anne. "I'll walk you home." And she did.

CHAPTER 10

Boy trouble.

So far, the Baby-sitters Club had managed to keep boys and boy trouble pretty much out of the meetings.

But not on Monday, October twenty-seventh. At that meeting, we were trying to discuss baby-sitting problems, but the subject of boys kept coming up instead. Kristy started it.

"Do you know what Alan Gray did to me today?" she asked, a look of pure disgust on her face.

"What made you think of Alan Gray?" I asked. We'd been talking about Charlotte Johanssen.

"Everything makes me think about him," said Kristy, throwing her hands in the air. "He bothers me all the time, every single second of every single day."

"He's not bothering you right now," said Mary Anne.

"Yes, he is. He bothers me just by living. Alan Gray is so horrible whenever he's around me, that he's all I can think about."

"So what did he do to you today?" asked Stacey.

"He hid my math homework, and then when it was time to hand it in and I couldn't find it, he jumped up and said to Mr. Peters, 'Excuse me, but I know where Kristy's paper is. Her little brother ate it. Kristy wouldn't give him breakfast and he was starving.' "

I giggled.

Kristy turned on me, eyes flashing.

"Well, I'm sorry, I think it's kind of funny."

"You would."

"Oh, Kristy," I said with a laugh. "Calm down."

"But it's not just that," she went on. (I could see that Kristy was determined to be upset.) "I think he's getting worse. On Friday he hid my shoes. On Thursday he called me a skinny pipsqueak in front of the class, and twice last week I caught him looking in my desk in the morning. Every day it's something. He never stops."

"Why don't you talk to . . . to Sam about it?" suggested Stacey.

"My own *brother?* No way. Besides, he'd never understand. He's girl-crazy. You should have seen who — or maybe I should say *what* — he took to the movies last Friday. She's a freshman in high school and she had spiky yellow hair with green stuff at the ends, and these little lace gloves with the fingertips cut out. Now, what is the point of wearing gloves if — "

Kristy stopped talking when she realized that the rest of us were staring at her.

"What? What is it?" she finally asked. Then she noticed Stacey, who was sitting on my bed, gazing sadly down at her hands.

"Sam took a high school girl to the movies?" she asked softly.

"Yeah, I — Oh, no. Stacey, I'm sorry." Kristy had forgotten all about Stacey's crush on Sam. "I'm sure it doesn't mean anything. He *is* interested in you. Really."

"Then what about that girl — "

"Tamara? You mean, why did he take her to the movies? Honestly, I don't know. But she was so weird, Sam'll never be serious about her. I'm positive. I think he went out with her just to shake Mom up."

"I thought he liked me," said Stacey.

"He does, he does," Kristy assured her.

"What do you mean when you say she's

weird?" asked Stacey carefully.

"Well, the green-tipped hair, for one thing. And the clothes. Her clothes were just . . . just *weird*."

"Like mine?" I asked suspiciously.

"Oh, no, not at all like yours," said Kristy, beginning to blush. *"Nothing* like yours."

I glanced at Stacey. For the first time since I'd met her, she didn't seem so sophisticated. In fact, she looked like a lost little girl. Two tears slid slowly down her cheeks.

"Oh, no! Please don't cry!" exclaimed Kristy.

Mary Anne jumped up from her spot on the floor and sat down next to Stacey. She can't stand for people to be upset.

The phone rang and I answered it. It was Mr. Willis from down the street. I'd baby-sat for his kids once before.

"Yes?" I said. "This Saturday? Sure, sure. . . . Eight P.M. . . . Sure. I'll be there." I hung up the phone and noted my job in our record book.

When I looked up, everyone was glaring at me, even Stacey. It was my turn to find out what I'd done wrong.

"Okay, what is it?" I asked.

"Did you just accept that job?" Kristy demanded.

I felt my stomach drop. "Yes," I whispered.

"But Claudia, you know the rule."

Of course I knew. I'd just forgotten. "I'm supposed to check with everyone else first."

Kristy nodded. "I'm free on Saturday."

"So am I," added Mary Anne.

"Oh," I said.

"I'm not," said Stacey, "but I wish you'd asked me. You didn't know I was busy."

"I — I'll call him back," I suggested. "One of you guys can have the job."

"No," said Kristy. "That makes us look disorganized. You keep the job. But I want to know something. How often do you get calls for the club and accept jobs without asking anyone else first?"

"Oh, not often. I mean, almost never. Only . . . only once before."

"That job with the Newtons?"

"All right, twice, then."

"You mean that job with Charlotte?" asked Stacey.

"Oh, all right, three times."

"Claudia!" exclaimed Kristy.

"I don't do it on purpose!" I exploded. "I'm not trying to cheat you guys, you know."

"We d— "

"It's just that I have so much on my mind."

"What's wrong?" asked Mary Anne.

"The Halloween Hop is only four days away

and I don't think Trevor even knows my name yet."

"Wow," said Stacey sympathetically. "I didn't realize it was getting that serious."

I nodded. "I guess there's no hope now."

"Yes, there is!" Mary Anne cried suddenly. "Where there's time, there's hope! And you've got four days. Anything could happen in four days."

"I think you should talk to him," said Kristy.

"*I* think you should ask him to the dance," said Stacey.

I gasped. "No way! This isn't the Sadie Hawkins dance. I can't ask a boy to go with me."

"In New York we did it all the time."

"Well, this isn't New York. It's little Stoneybrook. And I am not asking Trevor Sandbourne to the Halloween Hop."

"You're scared," said Stacey.

"You're right."

"Maybe Trevor is scared, too."

"You think so? He *is* sensitive. . . ."

Before Stacey could answer, the phone rang again.

"*I'll* get it," said Kristy meaningfully, reaching for the receiver. "Hello? . . . Hi, Mr. Newton. Where are you? At the office? . . . Oh. . . . *Oh.* . . ."

"What?" I asked.

Kristy waved at me to be quiet. "Now?" we heard her say. "But I thought the baby wasn't due for three more weeks. . . . Oh. . . . Mmhmm. . . . Jamie called you? . . . I didn't know he could use the phone, either. . . . Yes. . . . Right. . . . Okay, we'll be here. 'Bye."

"The baby?" squealed Mary Anne. "Already?"

"I guess so," replied Kristy. "Mr. Newton said that Jamie just called him at the office and said he wanted him to come home. When Mr. Newton asked if the baby was on the way, Jamie said yes!"

"Oooh! I can't believe it!" I cried.

"So Mr. Newton says he'll probably need one of us to stay with Jamie this evening. If he's going to be at the hospital really late, Jamie can just spend the night at our house, I guess. He's done that once before. Mr. Newton will call as soon as he gets home."

"Gosh, I hope Mrs. Newton's all right," said Stacey. "I mean, asking Jamie to call Mr. Newton, and the baby coming early and everything."

"Yeah, you're right," I said.

For a moment we forgot our boy problems.

"Are babies who are born three weeks early usually okay?" I asked.

The other members of the Baby-sitters Club shrugged. "Don't know," said Mary Anne.

"I once heard of a baby who was born three *months* early," said Stacey. "He had to stay in the hospital practically forever, but now he's okay."

"David Michael was two weeks early," put in Kristy, "and he was just a little small. The doctors made him stay in the hospital three extra days to gain a few more ounces, but he was fine."

"You know something?" said Mary Anne. "I don't even know whether I was born early or late or on time. Dad hardly ever talks about stuff like that — you know, what I did when I was a baby. It's times like this when I wish I had a mother. I bet she'd talk about those things."

For a moment nobody said anything. I saw Stacey looking sympathetically at Mary Anne. Stacey once told me she wished she knew her better, but Mary Anne is still a little shy when she's around Stacey.

Then Kristy broke the silence (as usual) and saved the day. "You know what?" she said to Mary Anne. "You should ask my mother those things. Or ask Mrs. Kishi or Mimi. I bet they'd know, since we all grew up together. My mom told me once that when we were really little, around a year old, our parents formed a play group for us, so we could be with kids our own age, and they could talk about child rearing and stuff. They must have known all three of us pretty well."

"Really?" asked Mary Anne. "Maybe I will ask one of them . . . some day."

The phone jangled. "Mr. Newton!" cried Kristy, as she dove for the receiver. "Baby-sitters Club," she said officially, and I realized I'd forgotten to do that earlier. Another strike against me. Kristy nodded at us to let us know that it was Mr. Newton on the phone. We watched her face anxiously. "It was?" she said, looking disappointed. "Oh . . . oh. . . . Sure, we understand. Actually, I'm glad the baby's not coming early. It'll be better for him — or her — to be on time. . . . Right. . . . Right. No problem. Okay, see you soon. 'Bye." Kristy hung up the phone.

"False alarm?" I asked.

"You could say that." Kristy began to giggle.

"What's so funny?"

"Mrs. Newton is fine. She didn't even know Jamie was using the phone. You know how Jamie always wants to talk to his dad and waits for him to come home from work every day?"

We nodded.

"Well, today he got tired of waiting and just

went ahead and called his father for a chat. Mrs. Newton had taught him how to dial the number in case there ever *was* an emergency with the baby or something, only Mr. Newton didn't know that. Anyway, Jamie told Mr. Newton he wanted him to come home — because he always wants him to come home — and Mr. Newton asked if the baby was on the way, and Jamie said yes — because of course a baby *is* on the way in his house and — oh, it was just a big mix-up!"

We all began to laugh.

"It'll be pretty exciting when the baby really does come," said Mary Anne.

"It would be pretty exciting if Trevor asked me to the dance," I added. I sighed loudly.

If I had known what was going to happen that very night, I might not have bothered sighing over Trevor. He was nothing compared to the other problems that were about to come up.

CHAPTER 11

After dinner that night, it was Mimi's turn to help me with my homework.

"Mostly math," I told her ruefully as we settled ourselves at the kitchen table. "We're having a test on Thursday and Mr. Peters gave us review problems. Plus, he gave me extra work. Only me, Mimi. No one else," I grumbled.

"And what is this work, my Claudia?"

"Memorizing the times tables. Mr. Peters knows that someone helps me with my homework, and he said for me to drill tonight. You're supposed to go through the deck of flashcards twice with me. Boring, boring. I haven't done that since fourth grade."

"It is just a review, my Claudia. The memorization helps. When you know the tables just like that" — Mimi snapped her fingers — "your math will go much faster."

"Well, I like anything that makes it go faster."

Mimi smiled. "All right. We will go right through the deck. The cards are not in order." She held one up. "Six times seven."

"Forty. I mean, forty-two."

"Eight times three."

"Twenty-four."

"Good girl."

We were about halfway through the box when the doorbell rang. Mimi knew I needed a break. "Why don't you answer the door, my Claudia?"

I leaped to my feet. When I reached the door, I peeped out the front window to see who was there, and was surprised to see Mr. and Mrs. Goldman from next door. They're an older couple who don't have any children and travel a lot, so we don't see much of them. As far as I could remember, they'd never come over without calling first.

"Mom!" I yelled as I unlatched the chain. "Dad! It's the Goldmans."

"Hi," I said, opening the door.

"Claudia, dear," said Mrs. Goldman. She was clutching her husband's arm and looked terrified.

"We're sorry to disturb you," Mr. Goldman said.

My parents appeared behind me. "Eileen, Arnold," said my mother. "Please come in. Is anything wrong?"

The Goldmans stepped into the foyer. "We think we've been robbed," said Mr. Goldman shakily. "We went out to dinner and when we came back just now, the front door was open a crack — "

" — and I'm positive I left a light on in the living room," said Mrs. Goldman tearfully, "but the house is dark."

My heart began to pump faster. It sounded as if it were beating right in my ears.

"We were afraid to go inside," said Mr. Goldman. He was twisting his hat practically into knots.

"We're glad you came over," said my mother. "I think it was wise not to go in the house. You just never know." She patted Mrs. Goldman's arm.

"I'll call the police," said Dad.

"And I'll fix some tea," added Mimi, who had joined us.

Two policemen showed up quickly, before Mimi even had a chance to pour the tea. They listened to the Goldmans' story, then went next door to check the house. When they returned, one said, "Well, I'm afraid you *have* been robbed. The place is a bit messy upstairs.

However, the intruder, or intruders, is gone now. I think you can return safely."

Mr. Goldman nodded.

"Tell me, sir," said the younger policeman, "did anything unusual happen today? An odd phone call, anything like that?"

Mr. Goldman shook his head. "No, I d— "

But his wife interrupted him. "Wait. There *was* a funny call, Arnold. Two, actually. They came when you were working in the cellar." She turned to the policemen. "He has a wood-shop down there," she explained. "Late in the afternoon the phone rang. When I answered it, I said hello twice, and then the caller just hung up. It happened again about a half an hour later."

I knew my eyes were opening wider and wider. "The Phantom Caller," I croaked.

The young policeman looked at me sharply. Then he nodded ever so slightly at his partner.

Well, as you can imagine, I had to get on the phone immediately and begin telling people about the Phantom. The first person I called was Stacey. I could almost hear her jaw drop.

"What did he get?" she squeaked.

"A pearl necklace and a gold brooch. Both very valuable. The brooch was an antique."

"I just don't understand," said Stacey. "How does he know?"

"Beats me. The police did say one interesting thing, though."

"What?"

"They said they're not sure this robbery fits the Phantom's pattern. They said it may be a copycat crime. You know, just some local punk who wanted to get a little fast cash and is covering his tracks by disguising the crime as the Phantom's. The police said they were very surprised to see the Phantom working a neighborhood like ours."

"What's that supposed to mean?"

"It means usually he sticks to millionaires."

"Oh."

After I talked to Stacey, I got on the phone with Kristy and told her the news. She said she would call Mary Anne. Then Mimi made me return to my homework. We were almost finished with the flashcards when the phone rang. Mimi answered it, then handed it to me. "It is Kristy," she told me. "Please speak only for a few minutes."

"Okay. Thanks," I said, smiling at Mimi as she handed me the receiver. Mimi is the only one who lets me take phone calls during the homework sessions.

"Claudia," said Kristy, not even answering my hello, "we have a big problem."

"What?" I asked with a groan.

"I should never have told Mary Anne about the Goldmans, although she would have found out anyway."

"What happened?"

"She told her father about the robbery and he's forbidden her to do any baby-sitting until the Phantom is caught."

"Oh, no."

"And she's got three jobs lined up this week."

"Oh, *no*."

"Yeah. I think her father is actually just mad that she was on the phone after dinner and not discussing homework. You know his silly rule."

"I know."

"But we still have to cover for her. I'm calling an emergency club meeting during recess tomorrow."

"Okay. I'll see you in school." We hung up.

When we finally finished my homework, Mimi came upstairs and sat for her portrait again. I was working on her eyes, which were the hardest part for me. When Mimi looks at me, I see all sorts of things expressed in her eyes. I wanted very badly to show that on the canvas, and it was difficult.

"How are you and Janine getting on?" asked Mimi, remembering the conversation we'd had the last time she'd posed for me.

"The same," I said.

"You know, my Claudia, that in order for things to change, *you* must change them. You will grow to be an old woman like me, if you wait for others to change things that do not please you."

I thought about that. I thought about the times Janine had tried to talk to me and I had brushed her off. I thought about the times I had been cross with her, without telling her why I was cross. But all I said to Mimi was, "When I'm an old woman, I hope I'm just like you."

Mimi smiled.

I added flecks of light to the pupils in Mimi's portrait, and her eyes looked almost right.

The next day, school was buzzing about the Goldmans' robbery. Word had spread quickly. Was it the Phantom or not? Had he really come to Stoneybrook? Should our parents buy fancy alarm systems for our houses? Should we put our valuables in safe-deposit boxes at the bank?

The one thing everyone agreed on was that if the robber really was the Phantom, we didn't have anything to worry about *personally*. He usually only struck when a home was empty, and he had never injured anyone. No one had even seen him.

I spent math class that day trying to design a plan of attack on Trevor Sandbourne. It was Tuesday. The Halloween Hop was on Friday, just three days away. I knew that I could not, as Stacey had suggested, ask *him* to the dance, but I could try to attract his attention, get him to notice me.

At noontime, I bought the hot lunch — meat loaf, green beans, and mashed potatoes (all prime candidates for a food sculpture). Dessert was — what else? — red Jell-O. As I was walking toward the table where Stacey, Dorianne, Emily, and the boys were sitting, I noticed Trevor just a couple of tables away from them.

Aha, I thought. I can start doing something to get Trevor to notice me. I decided to take a shortcut to my table, which would involve squeezing by Trevor. Maybe I could say hi to him while I was at it.

I approached him, holding my tray tightly. Trevor was sitting at the end of his table. I squeezed around behind him, and just as I did so, the kid seated in back of Trevor stood up suddenly. I lost my balance — and my plate of Jell-O slid off my tray and landed Jell-O-side-down in Trevor's lap. Very slowly, he looked at it, then at me, while red stuff oozed to the floor.

His face turned as red as the Jell-O.

I knew mine was red, too.

What I didn't know was what I was supposed to do. Every kid at Trevor's table was staring at me. A bunch of other kids were staring, too. At long last I balanced my tray on one knee, handed Trevor my napkin, and said, "Sorry. I'm sorry." Then I fled to an empty seat next to Stacey. I crumpled into the chair and buried my face in my hands. "I am *so* embarrassed," I whispered. "Is everyone still looking at me?"

Stacey glanced around. "No. They're watching Trevor clean up his pants. By the way, you left the Jell-O plate in his lap."

"Oh, no. Oh, no."

"Hey, good going, Claudia!" Rick exclaimed.

"Yeah, that was really coordinated," added Howie.

"Shut up, you guys," I said. My face was still flaming.

"Oooh, touch-*ee*," said Pete.

Honestly, boys can be such pains. Well, some boys can be. Rick, Howie, and Pete would probably bring this incident up periodically until we graduated from high school. Maybe for the rest of our lives.

I decided that I would try to paint a picture about embarrassment. The main color would be red.

I was glad that we needed to have an emergency meeting of the Baby-sitters Club because it helped me to forget that I had just blown the Halloween Hop and would be sitting at home like Kristy and Mary Anne on Friday night. *They* didn't care about not going to the dance, but I sure did. (Stacey, I happened to know, was going to be invited to the dance by Pete. Pete had told Rick, who'd told Howie, who'd told Dorianne, who'd told me. And Dorianne and Emily were both going to go.)

Kristy gathered the club members beneath an unused basketball hoop on the playground. Before she could even open her mouth, Mary Anne spoke up. "I just want to tell you guys that I'm really sorry. This is all my fault. I'm causing problems and I feel terrible."

"It's not you, it's your father," said Kristy.

"I know, but you three have to take over all my work."

"Don't worry about it," said Stacey.

"That's right," I added. "Every business faces problems sometimes. Mimi says that

116

solving problems strengthens character."

Mary Anne smiled. "Mimi is usually right."

"Okay," said Kristy, rubbing her hands together. "Let's get to work." She opened our appointment book, which she'd been carrying under one arm. "Hmm. Mary Anne, you're supposed to be sitting for the Marshalls for an hour this afternoon, for Claire and Margo Pike tomorrow, and for Charlotte Johanssen on Saturday morning, right?"

"Right."

"Well, let's see. Today is usually my day to watch David Michael, but I switched with Sam since Claudia and I are sitting at the Newtons' starting at five this afternoon. If Mrs. Marshall really just needs someone from three-thirty to four-thirty, I could do that."

"Okay," said Mary Anne. "Here, let me take the book and keep track of all this stuff. It's my job, anyway."

Kristy handed the book over.

"Now," said Mary Anne. "Let's take care of the Pikes. Claudia, you're not down for any jobs tomorrow."

"No, but I have my art class."

"Oh, right."

"I could skip it," I said reluctantly.

"No, I'll take your job, Mary Anne," said Stacey.

"But you're down for Charlotte."

"Oh, not anymore. Dr. Johanssen called last night to cancel. I didn't have a chance to change the book."

"Great. Okay, the Pikes are taken care of. That leaves Charlotte on Saturday. How come Dr. Johanssen canceled tomorrow? Maybe she'll cancel Saturday, too."

"I don't think so," said Stacey. "It was just that some meeting was called off tomorrow. It's not going to affect Saturday."

Mary Anne sighed. She looked at the book again. "Claudia?" she asked.

"Sure, I'll watch Charlotte."

Mary Anne snapped the book shut. "I've been thinking," she said firmly. "I shouldn't be part of the Baby-sitters Club anymore."

"*What?*" Kristy and Stacey and I cried.

"It's not fair," Mary Anne went on. "Who knows how long it'll be before the Phantom is caught. Dad could keep me on baby-sitting probation for years."

"But — but — " said Kristy.

"Hey, I've got an idea!" I cried. "Why don't you stay on as secretary of the club. You keep all our records and appointments so neatly. Nobody else will do as good a job."

"Well . . . " said Mary Anne. "But I'm not going to be earning any money. I might not

118

be able to pay my club dues."

"Let's not worry about that now," said Kristy.

"Right," I added. "Us baby-sitters have to stick together. Through thick and thin."

"Through Phantoms and power failures," said Stacey.

"Through fires and floods," said Kristy.

We put our arms around each other and headed into the school building just as the bell rang.

CHAPTER 12

Late that afternoon, Kristy and I began one of our most terrifying baby-sitting experiences ever. Jamie Newton's mother had called two weeks earlier needing a sitter for that evening. There was one hitch: Jamie would not be the only child at the Newtons'. His wild cousins would be there, too. I'd baby-sat for them once before — by myself — and based on that experience, I told Mrs. Newton she would need two sitters the second time, especially since the job was over the dinner hour and the kids would need to be fed.

Jamie's cousins were Rob, Brenda, and Rosie. Rob, the oldest, was eight; Brenda was five; and Rosie was three. And they were tough to handle. Rob hated girls (including girl baby-sitters), Brenda was fussy, and Rosie was noisy. Well, they were *all* noisy. The other time I had sat for them, they jumped and ran around the living room and disobeyed practically everything I said. I had finally managed to calm them down, but I still wasn't looking forward to the evening, although it was bound to be different with Kristy there.

We arrived at the Newtons' at five o'clock and found the place already in chaos. The adults, Jamie's parents and Mr. and Mrs. Feldman (the parents of Rob, Brenda, and Rosie), were trying to get ready to leave, but three of the four kids (all but Rob) were crying, Mrs. Feldman couldn't find the sandwiches she'd brought for our supper, and Mrs. Newton suddenly discovered that her good coat wouldn't button around her middle anymore.

"Darn," she said. "I wore this coat the entire time I was pregnant with Jamie. I just don't understand it."

"Sis?" called Mrs. Feldman from the kitchen. "The sandwiches absolutely are not in the refrigerator. If they are, they're invisible. . . . Rosie, stop it. I don't know why Brenda hit you."

"Not that refrigerator. I put them in the one in the basement," Mrs. Newton called back. "Get Jamie to show you. . . . What am I going to wear tonight? I can't wear that awful maternity coat, not to *this* cocktail party. . . . Roger?" she shouted upstairs to Mr. Newton.

"Mommy." Jamie came sniffling into the hall

and pulled on his mother's hand. "I don't want to go in the basement with Aunt Diane."

"Never mind, Sis. I found them. . . . Brenda, *stop* it. You're pestering your sister."

Well, things went on that way for about five more minutes, but finally Mrs. Newton found a shawl to wear instead of the coat, and, miraculously, Jamie, Brenda, and Rosie stopped crying.

The adults left.

Kristy and I looked at each other, then at the living room where the four kids were standing.

They eyed us and we eyed them.

Rob gathered his sisters in a huddle while Jamie looked on.

Suddenly the huddle broke and the Feldmans began tearing and screaming and jumping around, just as they had done when I sat for them before. That time I had ignored them, and after a while they'd quieted down.

But Kristy had a different idea. You have to remember that even though she's small for her age, she's a tomboy, and she's used to boys and a big family.

The Feldmans hadn't been screeching and tearing through the living room for more than three seconds, when Kristy put her fingers in her mouth and blew — hard. An ear-piercing whistle screamed from her lips.

The Feldmans stopped cold.

"Now hear this!" shouted Kristy. "No yelling, no running, and no jumping inside this house — and I mean it." She saw that Rob was about to say something, so she added, "One false move and I'll punch your lights out. That goes for all of you. Do you hear me?"

The Feldmans nodded.

Jamie was wide-eyed with disbelief at what his beloved Kristy had just said.

"Do you understand me?" she went on.

The Feldmans nodded.

"Any questions?"

Rob started to open his mouth again, then thought better of it and raised his hand instead.

"Yes?" said Kristy.

"How did you do that?"

"Do what?"

"Whistle with your fingers."

"Oh. Here, I'll show you. But if you learn how to do it, remember that this is usually an outdoor whistle, not an indoor one. Got it?"

"Yes."

Kristy took Rob into the basement for whistle practice and I led the three younger children into the rec room. I had just settled them into one of Jamie's favorite activities — coloring pictures of monsters — when the phone rang.

"I'll get it," I called down to Kristy. I dashed into the kitchen. "Hello, Newtons' residence."

Nothing. I couldn't hear a sound.

"H–hello?" I tried again.

It's funny how sometimes you can be just as scared by *nothing* as by *something*. My hands were shaking as I hung up the receiver.

"Who was it?" called Kristy.

"Wrong number," I replied uneasily. I didn't want to frighten any of the kids, but considering what had happened to the Goldmans the night before, I suddenly thought I had good reason to be nervous.

As soon as possible, I would tell Kristy about the call in private.

A half an hour later, just as I was beginning to think about supper, the phone rang again.

Kristy was coming up the stairs with Rob, who looked very proud of himself. "I'll get the phone this time," she said.

I nodded and followed her into the kitchen. "Hello?" she said. "Hello?"

I could tell immediately that it was another one of *those* calls.

Kristy hung up the phone, looking nervous. I glanced into the rec room to make sure all the kids were busy. "No one there?" I asked Kristy.

She shook her head.

"The first call was like that, too. It wasn't really a wrong number."

Kristy bit her lip. "What do you think?" she whispered. "Is it time for the Phantom to strike again?"

I shrugged. "Do you think it could be Sam goof-calling?" Kristy's brother had quite a reputation. And he liked to give the Baby-sitters Club a hard time every now and then.

"It's possible," said Kristy thoughtfully. "He's pretty interested in this Phantom business, but it's not like Sam to call and not say anything. He kind of likes to leave his mark, if you know what I mean. It'd be more like him to get on the phone and say in a really spooky voice, 'Woooo, Kristeee. Phantom here. Woooo, you better hide your plastic ring and your charm necklace, because I'm on my way over. . . .' "

I smiled in spite of things. "Well, look. If it *is* the Phantom, we're safe because he probably won't rob the house if someone's in it."

"He might. He has before. Besides, we're just kids. Maybe he figures — "

"He can't figure anything. He doesn't know whether any adults are home. Just because we answered the phone doesn't mean — "

And at that wonderful moment, the phone rang a third time. I snatched it up, saying, "Hello? . . . Hello?" Then on inspiration, I shouted into the kitchen, "Hey, Dad, it's another funny call. I think — "

The caller hung up before I could finish saying, "I think we better phone the police." I smiled nervously at Kristy as I put the receiver down. She smiled nervously back at me.

"Well," she said briskly, "let's start supper. I bet the kids are hungry."

"Anyone want dinner?" I called into the rec room. Peace was still reigning there. I almost hated to disrupt it. But one of our responsibilities as baby-sitters that night was to feed Jamie and the Feldmans.

"Starving!" Rob shouted, jumping up.

"Yes!" chorused the others. They dropped their crayons and ran.

"Whoa," I said. "Everybody back in the rec room and put the crayons and paper away."

"*I* wasn't coloring," said Rob.

"You can set the table then," I told him.

"All right," he agreed cheerfully.

A little while later the table was set. Mrs. Feldman's sandwiches were stacked on a plate in the middle, the glasses were filled with milk, and Kristy and I were passing around apples and oranges. It was a simple dinner, and everyone, including Kristy and me, seemed happy with it.

In fact, we were so happy that for a few

minutes we ate in silence. All I could hear were crunchings and munchings and Jamie gulping his milk.

And a little bang from outside.

My eyes met Kristy's over the tops of our tunafish sandwiches. *Did you hear anything?* I asked her silently.

"Did you hear something?" Rob asked at that moment.

"Oh, probably just the wind," I replied, but my voice was shaking.

"There's no wind tonight," he said.

Another bang, not too loud.

"There it is again," he said.

"Maybe some dog is in one of the trash cans," suggested Kristy.

"Uncle Roger's trash cans are plastic."

"Well," I said bravely, "I'll just go check things." But I hadn't gotten any further than the living room (with Kristy and Rob at my heels), when we distinctly heard noises at one of the front windows and saw a shadow dart away into the falling darkness.

"That does it," I said, suddenly more angry than frightened. "I'm going to call the police."

And I did.

CHAPTER 13

The woman who answered the phone when I dialed 911 was very nice and very helpful. Obviously, she'd been trained to calm down people who were upset.

"Hello, hello!" I said, wishing it were possible to whisper and scream at the same time.

"Yes?" said the woman. "May I help you?"

"I'm baby-sitting," I whispered, "and there's a prowler outside. He was at the front window. We've been getting funny phone calls, too. The kind where the caller hangs up as soon as you answer."

"Okay," she said. "It's a good thing you called. What's your name?"

"Claudia Kishi," I replied.

"And what's the address of the house where you're baby-sitting?"

Thanks to Kristy, I was armed with that information. It was one of her new safety rules about baby-sitting: Always memorize the address and phone number of your client.

I gave her the address. "Thank you," she said, "and your phone number, too, just in case I need to call you back."

I gave her the number. "Very good. A car is already on its way over. It's just a few streets away and should reach you shortly. In the case of a prowler, though, we don't want to scare him off, so the squad car will park a little distance down the street. Then one officer will search the yard quietly, while the other will come to the door to talk to you."

"Okay," I said, glancing uncertainly outside. It was pretty dark out there. "How will I know it's a policeman at the door?"

"That's a good question. I can tell you're a smart baby-sitter. When the bell rings, ask who's there. The man will identify himself as an officer. Does the door have a chain lock?"

"Yes."

"Slide it shut right now — "

"Kristy, go put the chain on the front door," I hissed. She ran off.

" — and after the officer has identified himself, open the door just wide enough to see the badge he'll be holding out, okay?"

"Yes," I said. "Thank you. Oh, there's the doorbell. Thanks, thanks," I said hurriedly. I hung up.

Kristy was about to open the door. "Wait," I said, "let me take care of this. The lady told me what to do."

I dashed to the door, aware that Kristy, Rob, Brenda, Rosie, and Jamie had crowded behind me. I was glad. I needed their company.

"Who's there?" I called.

"It's Officer Drew."

After checking to make sure the chain lock was in place, I opened the door a crack. On the Newtons' stoop, bald head glistening under the porch light, stood an elderly man in a cop's uniform. He looked very nice, kind of like a grandfather, and very official, but he did not look like a policeman. At least, he did not look like my idea of a policeman. However, he was holding out his badge and some kind of I.D., plain as day. I glanced over my shoulder at Kristy. "Psst. Check him out," I whispered. I moved aside and Kristy peered through the crack.

"Who phoned in this — this complaint?" she asked, very businesslike.

"A Claudia Kishi," the man said patiently. "Would that be you?"

"No, it's me," I said from behind Kristy. "It's all right then, Kristy. Let him in."

We opened the door.

And I got the biggest surprise of my life.

With the door opened wide, I could see that two people were standing on the walk below Officer Drew. One was another cop in uniform.

The other was Alan Gray!

Kristy gasped.

"Who's that?" asked Rob.

Kristy got over her surprise fast, and got ready to battle Alan. After all, they're old enemies. "Alan Gray, you darn, sneaking, rotten — "

"You know this young man?" asked Officer Drew, a smile playing on his lips.

"You bet I do!" cried Kristy. "His name is Alan Gray. He lives on Rockville Court, he's in seventh grade at Stoneybrook Middle School, and he's a — "

Alan's face was falling faster than a ruined souffle.

"That's all right, young lady," said Officer Drew. "I get the general idea."

"Where'd you find him?" I asked.

"Behind the rhododendron bush at the side of the house," replied the other policeman. "By the way, I'm Officer Stanton."

"Hi," said Kristy, Rob, Rosie, Brenda, and I.

"Can I wear your hat?" Jamie asked Officer Drew.

Officer Drew smiled and handed his hat to

Jamie. "Could we come in for a minute? I think we have a few things to discuss."

I glanced at Kristy. She was fuming. Her eyes probably could have burned holes right through Alan. "Sure," I said.

Kristy made a face at me.

"Well, I *have* to let them in. They're the po*lice*," I whispered to her, as Jamie and the Feldmans stepped aside to make room for the others.

We all sat down in the living room. "Hey, you guys," I said to our baby-sitting charges, "if you go back in the kitchen now and finish your supper quietly, I'll let you have Cookie Surprises for dessert."

"What are Cookie Surprises?" asked Rob suspiciously.

"If I tell you, they won't be surprises. But you'll find out if you finish your dinner — and stay in the kitchen," I added.

The kids ran back to the kitchen.

Alan, the policemen, Kristy, and I looked at each other.

Officer Drew was about to say something when Kristy let her mouth take over.

"Okay, Alan, spill it," she said. "Was that you at the front window?"

I saw a mischievous glint in Alan's eye,

indicating that he was about to say no. Then he glanced up and found Officer Drew and Officer Stanton glaring ferociously at him.

"Yes," he admitted.

"Did you call here three times this afternoon and hang up when Kristy or I answered the phone?" I asked.

Alan dropped his eyes. "Yes."

"You wouldn't, by any chance, have called me once when I was baby-sitting over on McLelland, would you have?" (That was Watson's house.)

"Yes," he mumbled.

"And a few times here on other days, and maybe once or twice when I was sitting on Rosedale Road?"

"Yes." Alan was whispering by then.

"But how did you know I was going to be at all those places?"

"And why were you harassing this young lady?" said Officer Drew in a tone so stern I practically saluted him. I think he was just trying to frighten Alan a little.

"Well . . . um . . . which question should I answer first?" Alan cautiously asked the policemen.

"Mine," said Kristy.

Officer Stanton raised an eyebrow.

I kicked Kristy on the ankle.

"Okay." Alan licked his lips. "You — you made it easy for me," he said.

"*I* did?" replied Kristy. "How?"

"Well, it was all right there in that notebook of yours."

"What notebo— You mean, our club *record* book?"

"I guess so. That thing you started bringing to school every day. I checked it each morning. It had all sorts of information in it. Times, addresses — "

Kristy slapped the heel of her hand against her forehead. " — and phone numbers," she finished for Alan.

He nodded.

"Alan, you are a *rat!*" she exploded.

(The vague rustlings and eating sounds from the kitchen stopped suddenly.)

"A huge, gigantic, smelly — "

"All right, simmer down, young lady," said Officer Drew. He turned to Alan. "How did you get hold of the book every morning?"

"I would . . . borrow it. From Kristy's desk when she wasn't looking. I mean, the book was so neat and easy to read."

(Thanks to Mary Anne.)

"Do you know that that was an invasion of privacy?" asked the officer.

"Well. . . . "

"Okay, okay, okay," said Kristy. "So you looked in the book. How come you wanted to scare me?"

"Well," said Alan again, "I didn't. I wanted to — to ask you something, but I just couldn't. . . . I didn't have the nerve. And I *couldn't* ask you in school."

"But you had the nerve to steal our book and spy on me, not to mention pull my hair, trip me, take my lunch, and make up stories about me to tell Mr. Peters."

"Son," said Officer Stanton in a more kindly voice, "what did you want to ask her?"

Alan mumbled something that nobody could understand.

"Louder!" shouted Rob from the kitchen.

"Finish your sandwich!" I yelled back.

"What, Alan?" asked Kristy, sounding nearly civil.

"I wanted to know if you'd go to the Halloween Hop with me."

If I were Kristy, my eyeballs would have fallen out of my head along about then. But Kristy just said, "Oh, gosh, is *that* all? Of course I'll go with you. . . . Thanks."

And at that moment, the Feldmans and the Newtons returned. They were home early.

CHAPTER 14

Needless to say, the grown-ups were pretty surprised to walk into the living room and find their baby-sitters talking with two policemen and a strange boy.

Mrs. Newton gasped and Officer Drew jumped up and helped her into a chair. "It's all right, ma'am," he said. "The girls had a little problem, but they handled it well. The children are fine."

"Thank goodness."

"They're in the kitchen eating dinner," I added.

Officer Drew was eyeing Mrs. Newton's round belly warily. "Are you sure you're okay, ma'am?" he asked her.

"Just fine," she said breathlessly, "but Claudia, Kristy, what happened here?"

I looked at Kristy, hoping she'd want to explain. "He's *your* boyfriend," I whispered.

"*You* were the one who called the police."

I took a slow breath. Mrs. Feldman had gone into the kitchen to check on the kids, but Mr. and Mrs. Newton and Mr. Feldman were all ears. "Well," I began, "we got three strange phone calls after you left. We'd pick up the phone and the caller wouldn't say anything. And that was what happened to the Goldmans before they were robbed last night. Then, during dinner, we heard noises outside and when we went into the living room, someone was at the window. So I called the police."

"You did the right thing," said Mrs. Newton. "That was very responsible of you."

"Except that the prowler turned out to be *him*," I jerked my head toward Alan, "spying on Kristy."

"Well, you didn't know that," said Mr. Newton.

"I guess we'd better go now," Officer Drew said, standing up. "Let me just get my hat." At that moment, Jamie ran into the living room and handed it to him. "Thank you, young man. And *you*" — the officer turned to Alan — "are coming with us."

Alan turned pale. He swallowed noisily. "I am?"

"Is he in trouble?" asked Kristy.

"No, we're just going to give him a lift home. On the way, we'll have a chat about privacy and the proper use of the telephone. He can consider this a warning."

"Yes, sir," said Alan. As he followed the policemen out the front door, he glanced over his shoulder. "See you in school tomorrow, Kristy. 'Bye, Claudia."

" 'Bye," we said.

"Was he a bad boy, Kristy?" asked Jamie as soon as the door had closed.

"Just a little bit bad," replied Kristy.

"Hey, do we get Cookie Surprises or what?" Rob called to me from the kitchen.

"You certainly do. You were very good, all of you."

Kristy and I fixed the kids the dessert I had promised — chocolate-chip cookies with little scoops of ice cream on them. Then it was time to leave. Since it was dark out, Mr. Newton offered to drive us, but we live so close by that we said we'd walk. Besides, I wanted to talk to Kristy.

"So?" I said, when we reached the sidewalk.

"What?"

"Are you out of your mind? For years, you've hated Alan Gray. Hated his guts. You said so just a few weeks ago. And all we've been hearing since school started last month is how Alan's sitting in back of you is about as unfortunate as . . . as. . . . "

138

"As when they moved *The Love Boat* to ten A.M. so we couldn't watch the reruns anymore?"

"Yeah."

"I know. Well, it's just that Alan finally proved something my mother's been telling me for years. Only I didn't believe her until now."

"What's that?"

"That boys tease you because they like you. I have to admit that sometimes I still think Alan is kind of a jerk, and I wouldn't have minded if he'd gotten in a *little* trouble tonight. I mean, hanging around the window and frightening us with those phone calls. . . . He deserves to sweat, just like we did. However — Claudia, *a boy likes me.*" Kristy paused, then, looking mystified, went on, "Besides, he is sort of cute. And I guess some of the things he's done were funny . . . if you look at them a certain way."

I grinned at her. "Now you see how Stacey and I feel. That's why we sit at the lunch table with the boys. They like us. At least, they don't hate us. And it's pretty nice to be asked to a dance, isn't it?"

Kristy nodded, looking confused. "I don't quite understand all this," she said slowly. "I mean, how am I going to explain it to Mary

Anne? And, oh, gosh, can you imagine what my brothers will do when they see me getting ready to go to a *dance?*"

"Well, you can't back out now. Look, two nights from now, it will all be over. I think Mary Anne will understand. And Stacey and I will help you get ready before the dance. So don't worry."

We had reached our houses. "Thanks, Claudia," said Kristy. "I'll see you tomorrow."

" 'Bye." I sounded a lot more cheerful than I felt. As I crossed the street, all I could think was that Emily and Dorianne were going to the Halloween Hop, Stacey was probably going to the Halloween Hop (even though it would be with Pete Black, not Sam Thomas), Mary Anne didn't care about the Halloween Hop, and now Kristy was going to the Halloween Hop. And I wasn't. The boy I wished I could go to the Halloween Hop with didn't know anything about me, except that I had once dropped a plate of Jell-O in his lap.

I opened the front door to my house, let myself in, called hello to Mimi and my parents, and went to my room. I closed the door and lay down on my bed. Planning on being depressed for a while, I pulled a piece of saltwater taffy out of the stash in my pencil jar.

I was chewing away thoughtfully when someone knocked on my door. I didn't really want to talk to anyone, except maybe Mimi.

"Who is it?" I yelled.

"Janine."

Groan, groan. I wanted to talk to Janine less than I wanted to talk to a snake. "I can't talk now!"

"I think we'd better. This is urgent."

"Oh, all right. Come in." (Mimi would have been proud of me.)

Janine slipped into my room, closed the door quietly behind her, and perched at the foot of my bed. "What were the police doing at the Newtons'?" she asked me.

I popped another piece of taffy in my mouth before I had finished the first one. "Tap dancing," I managed to say.

"*Claudia. . . .*"

"How'd you know they were there?"

"Mrs. Gordon was giving me a lift home from the university and I saw the squad car driving away. I didn't think it could be too serious. There were no flashing lights. But I didn't tell Mom and Dad."

"You didn't?" I asked, feeling somewhat amazed. It's not that Janine is a tattletale, just that it's unlike her to be imaginative enough to think I might be in some kind of trouble that I wanted to cover up.

"No." Janine shook her head.

"Well, thanks," I said. "I mean, it's okay if they know. I'm going to tell them about it in a little while. But thank you for waiting to talk to me first."

Janine smiled and spread her hands, as if to say, No problem — which of course she wouldn't have said, not being one to use slang if she could help it.

"What did happen?" she asked. "Will you tell me first?"

"Sure," I said enthusiastically, sitting up. "Would you like a piece of taffy?" Remembering what Mimi had told me, I planned on making the most out of that sisterly, but unusual, moment.

"All right," said Janine.

I handed her a peppermint piece, and began telling her about Alan. "So then," I said, "I snuck — "

"Sneaked."

" — Whatever — into the living room, and someone was at the window!"

"What did you *do?*" she asked, her dark eyes shining.

"I called the police."

"You didn't scream?"

"Nope. Just went to the telephone." I told her the rest of the story.

"Gosh, you certainly were brave," Janine said appreciatively.

"I guess so," I replied. "I didn't feel brave at the time, though. I just knew that Kristy and I had to protect the children."

"I'm really proud of you."

"You are?"

"Yes. I'm proud you're my sister."

"Wow, I — Thanks. . . . Janine?"

"What?"

"How come you don't come to my room and talk to me like this more often?"

"Because you usually tell me to shut up or go away or mind my own business."

"Well, that's because you usually start talking like some big show-off professor. When we were little, we used to have fun. You talked like a kid."

Janine frowned. "Am I talking like a professor now?"

"No. But . . . but you're always telling me all this stuff I don't want to know, like how the fear process works. Who cares?"

"I do. Those things are interesting to me."

"Not to me."

"What is interesting to you?" asked Janine.

"Oh, mysteries and scary stories and baby-sitting and painting."

Janine nodded. "What happened tonight was exciting."

"Yeah!"

"I'm glad you let me come in and talk."

"Me, too," I said.

"Maybe we could do this more often?" Janine sounded a bit timid.

"Sure. I have a lot of other candy hidden around my room."

Janine smiled. "I'll tell you a secret. I do, too."

"You *do*?"

"Mm-hmm. It's my vice."

I wasn't sure what a vice was, but I wasn't about to ask. "I didn't know that."

"There are a lot of things you don't know about me."

"Same here."

"Well, let's go tell Mom and Dad what happened."

"Okay."

So we did. Mom and Dad and Mimi were pretty proud, too. After that, Janine gave me one final review for the math test the next day. She didn't seem to bug me as much as usual.

Everything was fine until I got into bed.

Then I thought of two things that made me feel sort of chilly all over. The first was that Trevor hadn't asked me to the dance.

The second was much worse. If Alan had been making the scary calls to Kristy over the past couple of weeks, then who had been making the calls to me? I'd gotten them several different times when I'd been baby-sitting, and the Phantom was still at large. . . . Was it possible, just possible, that he was after *me?*

No, I decided a few seconds later. It wasn't very likely at all. The Phantom went after jewelry, not people. And especially not people who didn't have any jewelry. How would Nancy Drew think if this were a mystery and she were the sleuth? I wondered. She would analyze the clues. She would review all her information.

Well, I thought, Kristy had received mysterious phone calls. I had received mysterious phone calls. Kristy's caller turned out to be Alan, a boy who secretly liked her. Maybe my caller was a boy, too! After all, Alan had looked in our record book. Maybe he had shown it to someone else.

Who could have a crush on me? Rick Chow? Maybe. Howie? I needed more clues.

I rolled over on my side and fell asleep.

* * *

The awful mystery was cleared up the next afternoon on what turned out to be a red-letter day. First, I took the math test. I worked very carefully and was the last kid to turn my test in. I wasn't sure how well I'd done, but I knew I had tried my best, which is not something I can say often.

But, boy, was I surprised when Mr. Peters found me at my locker at the end of the school day and said, "Congratulations, Claudia!"

"On what?" I asked warily.

"I started grading the test papers at lunch today. Yours was on top. I thought you'd like to know that you got an eighty-six."

"Really? An eighty-*six*? What is that, a B?"

"A 'B' or a B-plus, depending on how the rest of the class does. I can tell you've been working hard. It's really showing. Keep it up."

"I will, oh, I *will!* Thank you!"

As if that weren't enough excitement, I was baby-sitting for Nina and Eleanor Marshall a couple of hours later when the phone rang. I picked it up nervously.

No one was there.

"Darn," I said, as I replaced the receiver.

"What?" asked Nina.

"Oh, just a — a wrong number." Was it my secret caller? I actually began to hope the phone would ring again!

Immediately, it did. I grabbed up the receiver. "Hello? Who is this? Say something, *please!*" I waited, and after a moment an unfamiliar male voice said, "Claudia?"

I caught my breath. "Y–yes?"

The voice cleared its throat. "Um, this — this is Trevor. Trevor Sandbourne."

I very nearly fainted. "Nina," I whispered, placing my hand over the mouthpiece, "go get out the Sesame Street puzzles. I'll help you and Eleanor with them in a few minutes." I uncovered the phone as Nina and Eleanor ran off. "Trevor?" I said. I couldn't believe it!

"Yes. You . . . know who I am?"

"Oh, yes. I mean, of course I do. You're the poet. You write for *The Literary Voice.*"

"That's right," he said shyly. "What I was wondering is — I mean, I know this is last-minute, but could you — would you like to go to the Halloween Hop with me?"

This wasn't happening. It couldn't be. In a few minutes, I would wake up and find that the phone call was just part of a very real dream, like Dorothy's trip to Oz.

I pinched myself. It hurt. "I'd like to, Trevor. Thanks."

"You mean you can go?"

"Yes."

"Oh, good. I'll meet you there . . . at the

dance. Tomorrow at four, okay?"

"Okay. Trevor?" (I had to ask him.) "How did you know where to reach me? This isn't my house."

There was a pause at Trevor's end of the phone. "I sort of found out from Alan Gray."

"Aha."

"I — I know you know about Alan and the baby-sitting book. And, see, every time Alan took it, he'd check to see where Kristy'd be sitting . . . and then he would write down where *you'd* be sitting and give me the information. He knew I liked you. He caught me writing a poem about us once."

"A poem? About us?"

"Yeah. . . . "

"Do you still have it?"

"No," said Trevor sheepishly. "I threw it away. I was so embarrassed. Alan started singing some dumb song about kissing in a tree. Everybody heard him."

"So *that's* how he found out," I said.

"Yeah. Well, he felt bad about teasing me, since we're friends, so he began looking up your appointments for me. It was just his way of apologizing. . . . I guess now I owe *you* an apology. I'm really sorry, Claudia. Alan told me what happened last night. He didn't want to get me in trouble, so he didn't mention my name in front of the police. But when he got home, he phoned me and said I better straighten things out with you, no matter how sh— how hard it is for me. I'm sorry I've scared you with the phone calls. I really like you. I've been noticing you all year. I was just afraid to talk to you."

"That's all right, Trevor. I'm glad you finally did. I like you, too. I'll see you tomorrow."

I hung up the phone. I was going to go to the Halloween Hop after all! What a day!

"Hey, girls!" I called to Nina and Eleanor. "We're going to celebrate. Get your coats. I'll treat you to ice-cream cones!"

So we celebrated. We celebrated the happiest day of my life.

CHAPTER 15

The Halloween Hop was terrific. Kristy and Alan were there, and so were Stacey and Pete. Stacey looked as if she were having fun. Maybe Pete would help her forget about Sam Thomas. Mary Anne didn't go, and seemed quite happy about it.

On Thursday night, the night before the dance, Stacey and Kristy and I ran around to each of our houses as a group, trying on outfits for the others to approve. We had made a unanimous decision not to go in costume. We wanted to look nice. Besides, the boys had said they wouldn't be caught dead in costumes. Stacey and I ended up with baggy jeans and new bulky sweaters. We couldn't talk Kristy out of a plaid jumper and red turtleneck, but the next day, Alan didn't seem to care. When we got to the school gymnasium (after dashing home, changing out of our school clothes and into our dance clothes, then dashing back),

Alan met Kristy with a grin on his face that was as big as the ones on Trevor and Pete's faces.

After I hung up my coat, Trevor and I stood at the punch table and laughed about his phone calls and the Jell-O accident. When we ran out of things to talk about, we danced. To be honest, Trevor isn't much of a dancer and neither am I, but we had fun — lots of fun — anyway.

I had a new friend.

On the Monday after halloween, Mr. Peters handed back our math tests. My eighty-six had worked out to a B-plus. I gave my family the good news at dinner that night.

"Bravo!" said Dad.

"I'm so proud," said Mom.

Janine got up and actually gave me a little hug.

And Mimi smiled gravely and said, "I knew you could do it, my Claudia."

Two days later, the police caught the Phantom Caller — for real. They caught him in the act. A Mr. and Mrs. Johnson Neustetter, who lived in a house in Mercer that was more like a palace, got two of the Phantom's phone calls on Wednesday afternoon. The Neustetters had been following the accounts of the Phantom in the news, and alerted the police. On a hunch, the police staked out the Neustetters' that night. They arranged for the Neustetters to go out (figuring the Phantom was watching the house from somewhere). Sure enough, about twenty minutes after they'd left, the Phantom showed up. The police let him get into the house and all the way into Mr. Neustetter's safe before surprising him. He confessed to everything.

That night the Phantom was behind bars.

But guess whose mystery didn't get solved. The Goldmans'. The Phantom said he'd never been in Stoneybrook. So the police decided the Goldmans really had been robbed by a copycat thief. With the Phantom behind bars, though, no one would try that again. It would be too risky.

With that news, Mary Anne was back in the Baby-sitters Club. As soon as she and her father heard the news, Mary Anne begged to be allowed to baby-sit again and her father gave in.

We celebrated the capture of the Phantom at our next club meeting. I was ready with soda, a big bag of potato chips, another of peanut M&M's, and an apple and a package of crackers for Stacey.

"Well," said Kristy, tipping her head back and getting ready to drop a handful of M&M's in her mouth, "we survived the Phantom Caller."

"Yeah," I said. "This club can do anything."

"I've earned sixteen dollars in the last two weeks," said Stacey.

"I earned fourteen," added Kristy.

I opened up four cans of diet soda and handed them around.

"Here's to success," said Stacey.

"To us," said Mary Anne.

"To the Phantom," said Kristy, giggling.

"Here's to the Baby-sitters Club!" I cried.

We grinned, and clinked our soda cans.

About the Author

ANN M. MARTIN did *a lot* of baby-sitting when she was growing up in Princeton, New Jersey. Now her favorite baby-sitting charge is her cat, Mouse, who lives with her in her Manhattan apartment.

Ann Martin's Apple Paperbacks are *Bummer Summer, Inside Out, Stage Fright, Me and Katie (the Pest)*, and all the other books in the Baby-sitters Club series.

She is a former editor of books for children, and was graduated from Smith College. She likes ice cream, the beach, and *I Love Lucy*; and she hates to cook.